OBSOLETE

The Witch
of Maple Park

The Witch of Maple Park

by Stephanie S. Tolan

MORROW JUNIOR BOOKS

New York

Library of Congress Cataloging-in-Publication Data
Tolan, Stephanie S.
The witch of Maple Park/Stephanie S. Tolan   p.   cm.
Summary: Casey's friend Mackenzie is convinced that the
mysterious older woman she sees around town is a witch and that
she and Casey must do something to foil her.
ISBN 0-688-10581-5 (trade)
[1. Witches—Fiction. 2. Babysitting—Fiction. 3. Extrasensory
perception—Fiction.]   I. Title.
PZ7.T5735Wi   1992 [Fic]—dc20   92-7277   CIP   AC

To "the group":
Carole Adler, Athena Lord, Ruth Cotich,
Margaret Watson, Frank Asch, et al.
It was a good time.

1

It all started with a perfectly innocent phone call on a perfectly ordinary fall day. At least it was an ordinary day for my eighth-grade year at Maple Park Middle School. I was holed up in my room listening to the subliminal tape Mackenzie had promised would get me in touch with the math part of my brain.

That day, like almost every other day since school started, Mrs. Mendez might as well have been speaking Chinese in math class, for all I'd understood. I'd been put in eighth-grade algebra, an advanced class, because of my large vocabulary. If you know a lot of unusual words, school people think you're a brain who can do absolutely anything. Algebra was proving them wrong.

1

According to the booklet that came with Mackenzie's tape, there were math messages hidden under the sound of ocean waves, messages that were supposed to skip my ears and go straight to my brain to jump-start my "hidden math potential." The book said *everybody* has math potential. By listening to the tape twice a day for thirty days, I was supposed to start understanding Mrs. Mendez and pulling *A*'s—*B*'s at the very least.

For fourteen days, I'd been listening to waves. Nothing had happened yet. I was hoping I could speed up the process by listening twice as often. From now on, math was going to come first. I would listen to the tape day and night. I would not only conquer algebra, I would become an actual math whiz!

Right in the middle of listening to the tape my brother, Ian, bashed on my door. "Casey, phone!" he hollered, loudly enough to be heard over the ocean waves.

"Can't you read?" I yelled. "The sign says, 'Do Not Disturb!' " Now I would have to start the stupid tape all over again.

"It's Weirdo Mackenzie. If you want me to tell her you can't be disturbed—"

"I'm coming," I said, and untangled myself from my earphones. Ian calls Mackenzie names purely as a cover. If she were fifteen, the way she looks, instead of thirteen, he'd be all over her.

2

"Don't be long. I was talking to Wendy."

"Big whoop," I said to his slammed door. I wanted to keep it clear that Ian's busy love life does not impress me.

"Aren't you baby-sitting?" I asked as soon as I picked up the phone.

"Sure. I just thought it would be nice to have some non-three-year-old company for a change. Can you come to the park?"

"Well . . ." I thought about my math homework—ten problems I didn't know the first thing about solving. I thought about an *F* on my midterm report. "I'm listening to my math tape. I've got this humongous assignment—"

"You can get Ian to help you with it later," she said. "Come with us to the park now. Please?"

I wanted to say no. After all, I'd just decided math had to come first. And even if he helped with all my assignments, my sixteen-year-old brother probably didn't have what it took to find my hidden math potential. Only the tape could do that. *No,* I thought to myself, *I shouldn't go.*

But I've always had a hard time actually saying no to Mackenzie. And lately we didn't have much time together, what with school and her baby-sitting job. I could listen to the tape anytime. I could listen while I was doing dishes after dinner. And anyway, the booklet

3

might be wrong; I might not have any math potential at all. What if I was wasting all this time listening to boring ocean waves?

Mackenzie broke into the long silence. "Jonathan Thayer goes to the park sometimes to shoot baskets." So much for math. Mackenzie didn't even have to wait for my answer. "Meet us at the corner of Oak and Monument. Ten minutes." She hung up.

I pounded on Ian's door to let him know I was off the phone and then went back to my room to change into my favorite jeans and top, just in case Jonathan Thayer was at the park. I dragged my brush through my disgustingly curly hair, put on some lipstick, frowned at my hateful turned-down nose, and went downstairs. Like I said, everything seemed perfectly ordinary that day when I left the house.

2

Mackenzie has been my best friend since we were in kindergarten. Even way back then, everybody noticed her. She was always pretty—not cute, pretty. I can see it even in pictures of us eating ice-cream cones with melted ice cream on our faces, or running through the sprinkler with our hair all wet and scraggly. There was just something special about her.

Everybody is still noticing Mackenzie—boys, girls, teachers, everybody. Even if she wore ordinary clothes, they'd notice, because she's not just pretty anymore, she's gorgeous—tall and thin, with wavy chestnut-colored hair, even teeth, a perfect nose, and big, dark, piercing eyes. But she doesn't wear ordinary clothes.

Since the middle of seventh grade, she's been wearing huge wrinkled-looking Indian cotton shirts, dark baggy pants, and shoes made out of cloth, with rope soles. Her clothes are really weird for Maple Park Middle School. If I dressed like that, I'd get teased right out of the building. I figure she gets away with it because people cope with weirdness better in good-looking people.

Mackenzie and Barnaby were already on the corner when I got there. They made quite a pair. She was dressed in her usual baggy clothes and had her all-purpose baby-sitting tote bag on one shoulder. Barnaby Dawkins looks like a kid in a TV commercial, with jet black hair that curls around his face, bright blue eyes, and a perfect dimple in each round pink cheek. That day, he could have been advertising classy kiddie clothes. He had on a yellow and white checked shirt that matched the turned-up cuffs on his denim overalls.

He was stomping around and around Mackenzie and talking to the sidewalk. I watched him for a second and then looked at Mackenzie.

"He's walking Poo-doo," she explained.

"Ah," I said, nodding wisely. "Poo-doo."

"His dog."

"Ah." I really do not understand little kids.

"Let's go, Barn," she said to him. "We're off to the park."

"Let's go, Poo-doo," Barnaby said to the curb. He stamped his left foot and smacked his leg. "Heel!" he bellowed. But because he doesn't handle *l*'s very well, it came out more like "Hee-yew."

"He saw a TV show about dog training," Mackenzie whispered. "He's very serious about it."

We all waited for the invisible Poo-doo to get himself in position next to Barnaby's left leg, and then we headed down Monument Avenue. Barnaby stomped his high-topped sneakers on the sidewalk very hard and kept up a steady stream of chatter toward his ankle.

"Does he always stomp like that?" I asked quietly.

"It's supposed to remind Poo-doo to stay next to him."

"Makes sense," I said. "If a dog like that ran away, how would you find him?"

"Shhh."

It was impossible to compete with Barnaby's nonstop dog talk, so we didn't say much on the way to the park. I was mostly thinking about the possibility that Jonathan Thayer might be there. He's the most spectacular guy at Maple Park Middle School, and even though he never notices me, or even looks in my direction, I like watching him. A person can dream.

When we got to the playground at the park, there were a couple of guys bouncing a basketball around on the court, all right. But even from far away, it was obvious that neither one was Jonathan. They were too short. When we got closer, I saw that one was Howie Mankowitz, who sits next to me in math, and the other

7

was some seventh grader. Howie looked over at us when Barnaby stopped and shouted "Sit!" at Poo-doo. He grinned and waved. I gave him the smallest smile I could manage, just to be polite. Howie's nothing special, and anyway, I wasn't sure whether he was waving at me or Mackenzie.

The four Douglas kids who live down the block from me were on the playground. The older ones were fighting over the bouncy duck and the little ones, twins, were sitting in the sandbox, throwing sand at each other. Mackenzie pulled a shovel and dump truck from the tote bag. "Remember what your mother said, Barnaby," she told him as he rocked impatiently from one foot to the other. "Sand is for digging, not throwing."

"I bemember," he said. Mackenzie gave him his equipment. "Heel!" he told Poo-doo in a ferocious voice, and stomped off. He stopped when he got to the sandbox. "Sit!" he said. He put up his free hand, palm outward. "Stay!" He leaned down to pat the air and then climbed purposefully in and settled himself between the twins. Two seconds later, he was cheerfully heaving shovelfuls of sand at first one and then the other. They shrieked and threw sand back, until all three, eyes closed and spitting sand, were covered from head to toe. But nobody cried. Apparently among three-year-olds, this passes for a good time.

Mackenzie sat down on the bench to watch. I sat next

8

to her. "Shouldn't you stop them?" I asked.

"Baby-sitter's motto," she said. "Never disturb a happy kid. The sand'll brush off."

"You're the expert." I noticed that Howie kept glancing over at us between dribbles. I turned so that I couldn't see him anymore. It doesn't do my ego much good to watch people watching Mackenzie. It happens a lot, but she never seems to notice. "So," I said. "How come you wanted company today?"

Mackenzie sighed. "I've got a bad feeling, Casey."

When Ian calls Mackenzie weird, it's her clothes he's talking about. But the truth is, her clothes are only part of it. There's something else. It started two years ago when her father (she was always crazy about him and *thought* he was crazy about her) ran away with the anchorwoman from the "News at Noon" on Channel 8. They didn't actually run away; they just moved into a condo in Cincinnati. The divorce was nasty and very public. Afterward, Mackenzie's dad didn't visit and hardly ever even called. It was as if that newswoman had not only stolen him but was keeping him away from Mackenzie.

Mackenzie had a really rough time with the divorce. Her therapist got her started meditating as a way to reduce stress, and she got carried away. First it was just the meditation, which she did three times a day. Then it was a bunch of New Age stuff like crystals and "vibrations," and she started wearing those clothes. And somewhere in the middle of it all, she discovered she has psychic powers.

When she was doing her meditations, she started getting what she called *feelings*. The first one she told me about was when she and her mom were so broke that she couldn't afford to go up to Columbus on our class field trip. At first, she was all upset. Then, a few days before the money had to be turned in, she suddenly got all calm. "I've got a feeling. Something good is going to happen and I'm going to be able to go," she said. That very night, Mrs. Dawkins called and offered her the job baby-sitting Barnaby every day after school and on Saturdays. So she had money in time to go to Columbus. The job turned out to be good in other ways, too. Mackenzie is crazy about Barnaby. And all the time she spent with him was time she wasn't thinking about how awful her new stepmother was and how much she missed her dad.

That first feeling could have been a coincidence, but there have been lots of others. Sometimes the feelings are about little things, like in September when she knew ahead of time that three boys, including Jonathan Thayer, were going to invite her to the football dance. (That would have been a monumental thing to me, but it was a little thing to her because she had decided not to go at all. Ever since the divorce, except for Barnaby, Mackenzie has been pretty anti-male.)

Other times, the feelings are about big things. Like when she got a feeling that her mother's assistant was stealing from her business, Unicorn Catering. That's a long, complicated story, but the point is, her feeling turned out to be true then, too. There's a word for Mackenzie's feelings—*uncanny.*

"So what's this feeling about?"

Mackenzie sighed again, and I noticed for the first time that she was looking a little pale. There were shadows under her eyes. "It's Mom. And money. And Unicorn Catering."

"I thought everything was going so great," I said. Mrs. Brewster had started the business after the divorce, because she hadn't had a job before, and she and Mackenzie needed money. Things had been pretty rocky for a while, what with having to establish a reputation, and then the thieving assistant and all. But Mackenzie's mom was a great cook, so things had finally picked up.

"Everything was," Mackenzie said. "She was specializing in desserts, and people loved them. She makes the greatest desserts in the world."

Mackenzie didn't have to tell me. I've been eating at her house about once a week most of my life. I like her mom's chocolate éclairs best.

"But lately business has been really slowing down. People don't want all those big gooey desserts anymore. At least not *just* big gooey desserts. So she's been trying

11

to spread out, to do a little of everything. But she's not getting as many jobs as she was, and she's worried about money all the time. Dad is always late with the support payments, of course. *That woman* probably makes him spend all his money on her. And besides all that, Mom's second assistant got married and moved away. There's a new one—named Wanetta. Mom really likes her."

"That's good, isn't it?"

"It should be. But the bad feeling is about her, too."

"You don't think this one's stealing, do you?"

"No, no. I'm sure she's honest. But I don't think she's dependable. I've got a feeling she's not going to stay. Mom can't handle the business all by herself, even when things are slow. Besides, it feels as if the new ideas Mom's been trying aren't going to work."

Before I could say anything comforting, there was an earsplitting shriek. The oldest Douglas kid had smacked his sister in the mouth with a swing. Mackenzie got the damp towel she keeps in a plastic bag in her tote and wiped away the blood.

While she was doing that, Barnaby ran down the boy twin's sand castle with his dump truck and I had to get the truck out of the kid's hands before he could bash Barnaby over the head with it. Then the girl twin poked Barnaby in the eye with the shovel and he got two handfuls of her pigtails and started pulling. The racket

12

was amazing. Mackenzie had to help me pry the kids apart.

I was beginning to think playgrounds were a plot to rid the world of small children, but Mackenzie got everybody calmed down. Since Barnaby, she's gotten to be very good with kids. She could handle both the Douglas twins and the older kids, who were supposed to be taking care of them. We went back to the bench and I noticed the basketball court was empty. Howie and the other kid had left, probably because of all the screaming and crying.

"You're the only one I can talk to about this," Mackenzie said. "I don't want to worry Mom any more than she is already. She hasn't been sleeping much lately. I hear her in the middle of the night down in the kitchen. Or pacing in her room."

That explained the shadows under Mackenzie's eyes. If she was up listening to her mother, she wasn't sleeping, either. Maybe the bad feelings weren't psychic at all. Maybe she was just worried and tired. Everything always looks worse when you're tired.

Barnaby had left the sandbox now and picked up a stick. He waved it in the air and called Poo-doo to come and jump for it.

Mackenzie watched him gloomily for a few minutes, and then she smiled when he jerked the stick around as if he was snatching it away from Poo-doo's snapping

13

jaws. "That kid has some imagination," she said. Suddenly, she stiffened. I looked to see what she was staring at so intently.

Standing by the big oak tree near the swings, watching Barnaby, was a woman dressed in a long, flowing peasant dress in a blue and purple flowered print. Over the dress, she wore a bright orange and pink patchwork quilted jacket and under it bright purple tights and black running shoes. A purple hat with a wide floppy brim covered her head and part of her face. At first, I thought she was young, wearing those sixties hippie kinds of clothes. But the long, straight hair that hung down under the hat was white. Pure white. She carried a big black canvas bag over her arm. "That's one strange-looking old lady," I whispered.

"I've seen her before," Mackenzie said, her voice low. "A lot. It seems like everyplace we go, she turns up. Yesterday, when I took Barnaby to the library, she came into the children's room. And the day before that, she came to the fountain in the square while we were there."

"Well, you couldn't miss her," I said.

Mackenzie was staring at the woman, as still as if she were frozen in place. Barnaby backed toward the old lady, calling to Poo-doo to jump higher and get the stick away from him. The woman put her hands on his shoulders to keep him from bumping into her, and Mackenzie jumped up from the bench.

"Come on, Barn," she called. "I brought popcorn for the ducks. Let's all go over to the pond and feed them!"

The older Douglas kids whooped and headed for the path to the pond. The twins tumbled out of the sandbox and went after them.

The old woman let go of Barnaby. He turned and grinned up at her, then called Poo-doo and hurried toward us. Mackenzie retrieved her tote bag and moved purposefully away from the playground.

"Me and Poo-doo love the ducks!" Barnaby said.

Mackenzie shepherded Barnaby and Poo-doo ahead of her. I grabbed the dump truck and shovel out of the sandbox and followed, wondering what the big hurry was.

3

———————●———————

"I don't like this," Mackenzie said very quietly as we followed the path toward the duck pond.

Barnaby was stomping along in front of us, saying over and over in a loud voice, "Good boy, good boy, *heel* boy, good boy." Small children do not seem to be excessively bothered by repetition.

"What don't you like?" I asked, stuffing the shovel and dump truck into the canvas bag.

"That woman being every place we go."

"Maybe she just likes the same places you do."

"Like the children's room at the library?"

I shrugged. "Why not? Maybe she has grandchildren. Or maybe she likes kids' books."

"Don't you think it's a pretty big coincidence that she turns up in all those places at the same time we do?"

"What else could it be? You don't think she's following you or something."

"I don't know." Mackenzie patted Barnaby absently on the head as she walked. "She always seems to be watching Barnaby."

I looked down at Barnaby and couldn't help grinning. He was still stomping, still telling Poo-doo how good he was being. "Look at the kid," I whispered, so he wouldn't hear. "He's so cute, how could anybody not watch him?"

Mackenzie ran a hand through her hair. "Sometimes these feelings drive me crazy. I got another *bad* one back there, when she grabbed him—"

"She didn't grab him; she just kept him from crashing into her."

"I know, I know. But I saw those hands reaching for him and—Casey, the feeling just washed over me."

"It was probably a leftover from the other one—you know, about your mom's assistant and the trouble with the business."

Mackenzie shook her head. "This was different, Case. I felt there was something—I don't know—something *evil* about her."

"What's evil?" Barnaby asked. I hadn't noticed that he'd stopped talking to Poo-doo and was listening.

"Bad," Mackenzie said. "Wicked."

17

"You mean like a witch? Like a wicked witch?"

Mackenzie nodded. "Yes. Sort of like that."

Barnaby's eyes got even bigger than usual. "Is there a witch in the park?"

I laughed. I had a sudden vision of a witch on a broomstick swooping around over the sandbox.

"No witches here," Mackenzie assured Barnaby. "They're just in stories."

"Better not be a witch," Barnaby said, his lower lip jutting out. "I'd make Poo-doo bite her. I'd get a big stick and beat her all up!" But he grabbed for Mackenzie's hand and stayed right next to her the rest of the way down to the pond.

The ducks were mostly mallards, with a couple of big black and white ones with funny red growths around their beaks. They were clustered on the far bank of the pond when we got there. As soon as they saw us, they started quacking and waddling down to the water to swim over to meet us.

Mackenzie pulled out a plastic bag full of popcorn. Barnaby told Poo-doo to stay and took a handful. The Douglas kids came over to get a supply and the older ones went practically into the water with it, calling, "Duck, duck, duck." Pretty soon, we were surrounded by ducks, quacking and shoving to get at the popcorn.

I tossed kernels into the water, trying to get a few back to the shy little mallard who stayed away from the loud, bullying bigger ducks, and thought about Mackenzie's feelings. The ones she'd told me about had turned out to be true. But I didn't know if she'd told me about every single one. It would be easy to notice just the ones that did come true. Like those people who get a bad feeling about going on a plane and don't go and then the plane crashes. Afterward, they tell everybody they had a psychic warning. But probably they had feelings about other trips and went ahead anyway and nothing happened. They'd forget those times, wouldn't they?

Being psychic, even really psychic, didn't necessarily mean that every single thing you felt was real. If her mother's business was in trouble again, of course Mackenzie would have bad feelings. Anybody would, psychic or not. Between that and being tired—

I felt a jab at my toe and looked down. One of the big black and white ducks had tried to bite me through my sneaker. I dropped the last of my popcorn supply on the ground and moved away while he and three other ducks that had come up out of the water squabbled over it.

Mackenzie came over with the popcorn bag. "Look behind you," she muttered.

The old woman in the purple hat was standing about fifty feet away from us, watching the kids feed the ducks. My heart did a sort of double beat from the surprise of seeing her there so suddenly. "Lots of people come to watch the ducks at the park," I said.

Mackenzie gave the last of the popcorn to the oldest Douglas boy. "Come on, Barnaby," she called. He was standing in the middle of a cluster of ducks, holding out one kernel at a time and squealing when a duck snatched it from his hand. He didn't even look up. "Barnaby! We're going now!"

His face clouded over. "Not done!" he said. He held up his other hand to show he still had popcorn left. A big mallard, trying to shove another out of the way, knocked into him and the last of the kernels fell on the ground at his feet. The ducks almost pushed him over in their scramble to get them.

"Now you are," Mackenzie said. She waded in among the squabbling birds and took his hand. "Call Poo-doo. We're leaving."

Barnaby leaned away from her and braced his feet. "I wanna stay," he said, his face closed up like a fist. "I like ducks. Poo-doo likes ducks."

"We can go look for buckeyes," Mackenzie said, pulling his arm gently.

"I hate buckeyes," Barnaby answered. He didn't move.

"We can go to the square and get an ice-cream cone," she said.

"I hate ice-cream cones," Barnaby answered.

"I know where there's a buried treasure we could dig up," she said.

"I hate treasure," he said.

20

Mackenzie pointed to the ducks, which now were swarming around the Douglases. "Look, Barn, the ducks have all gone away. It's time for us to go, too." With that, she began walking, dragging him behind her. I grabbed the tote bag and went along.

We were about halfway from the pond to the sidewalk along Erie Avenue when Barnaby went limp and sank to the ground. Mackenzie stopped. She set him on his feet and he sank to the ground again. "Barnaby," she said, "stand up. What's the matter with you?"

"Poo-doo," he said. "He stayed with the ducks. We have to go back."

Mackenzie sighed. "Just call him. He'll come."

Barnaby sat on the grass and shook his head. His mouth looked as if it had been superglued shut.

"Look, here he comes now!" Mackenzie said. Barnaby looked where she was pointing and shook his head.

Mackenzie sighed. "Okay, Barn. Casey will go back to the pond and get Poo-doo. And then we'll all go to the pet shop and visit the guinea pigs."

Barnaby sat for a minute, thinking this over. "And the birds?"

"And the mice and the lizards and the fish."

"Okay."

So I had to go back to the pond and get Poo-doo. It was embarrassing. I had visions of Jonathan Thayer coming along just in time to see me pick up an invisible

21

dog and carry it away. The Douglas kids were still by the pond, but the old woman wasn't.

I didn't ask Mackenzie anything more about her feelings as we walked to the square. Bad enough Barnaby had overheard that business about evil and asked about a witch in the park. We didn't need a terrified three-year-old on our hands.

The only sounds as we walked the four blocks to Maple Park Square were Barnaby's constant chatter at Poo-doo about the animals we were going to see at the pet shop and the *stomp stomp* of his sneakers on the sidewalk. At the square, where Erie Avenue widens out and there's a little park in the middle with benches and a fountain, we passed the police/fire station, the jewelry store, and the health-food store and came to the Noah's Ark Pet Shop.

The window was full of the kinds of pet supplies only rich people (or goofy ones) buy for their animals—collars with rhinestones and little sweaters with matching booties, tea biscuits for dogs and tin boxes full of sardine-shaped crackers for cats.

A bell jingled as Barnaby pushed open the door and then held it for Poo-doo to follow him in. The warm, heavy smell of cages and aquariums greeted us. Tony, the mynah bird whose cage was just behind the door, gave an ear-piercing wolf whistle. "Hello, hello," he said in a deep man's voice.

"Hi, Tony," Barnaby said. He hurried past the wall

of fish tanks to the back, where the guinea pigs were kept in big cages behind glass. Mr. Pedersen, the owner, was busy at the cash register with a woman who held a tiny white puff of a dog under one arm. He waved as Barnaby tramped past and nodded to us as we stopped to pretend interest in a tankful of neon tetras.

"That wasn't a coincidence. The woman came after us," Mackenzie said.

"She just went to the pond to watch the ducks."

Mackenzie shook her head. "She was watching Barnaby. *My* Barnaby. I don't like it."

The woman with the puff of a dog went out. "Hello, hello," Tony said as the doorbell jingled. Mr. Pedersen came to ask if we wanted something.

"We're just waiting for Barnaby to finish looking," I said.

"I got in a beautiful pair of black gerbils today," Mr. Pedersen said. "Would the little guy like to see them?"

"I'm sure he'd love to see black gerbils."

Mr. Pedersen went back to show Barnaby the gerbils and I looked at Mackenzie. She had her eyes closed. I waited for a minute and she opened them again. "I was trying to see if I could get any other feelings about her," she said.

"And?"

"Nothing. I just keep seeing that purple hat. She's had it on every time we've seen her."

"There's nothing evil about wearing a hat." I

grinned, trying to make it a joke. "Not even a big purple one that clashes with your clothes. Weird, but not evil." Mackenzie didn't smile.

"I can't concentrate here." She looked at her watch. "It's time to get Barnaby home. Can you come to my house after? I want to meditate and see if anything comes clearer. You could try, too." Mackenzie's been trying to teach me to meditate, to see if I have any psychic powers. So far, it hasn't worked. "Then you could stay for supper."

I thought about those math problems. Ian would just *have* to help me with them. "I need to call Mom, but it's probably okay."

"Good." Mackenzie flipped her hair away from her face. Her jaw was set in a very determined way. "If there *is* something evil about her, we'll find out."

We went to the back of the store, where Barnaby was holding a black gerbil. His eyes were shining and he held his chubby hands very still as the gerbil sniffed his fingers. "Can I have him, 'Kenzie?" he asked, his voice low and careful so he wouldn't scare it. "Can I, please?"

Mackenzie shook her head. "You know what your mother says about pets. We can only come here to look."

Barnaby's chin quivered. He looked up at Mr. Pedersen and held his hands out. "Can't," he said.

Mr. Pedersen took the gerbil and ruffled Barnaby's

hair. "That's all right. You can come visit him here anytime."

"We have to go now," Mackenzie said. "Get Poo-doo."

We waited while Barnaby said good-bye to the gerbils, the cages of hamsters and mice, the snake and the tankful of lizards. Then he said good-bye to each guinea pig. Finally, he was ready. "Heel!" he commanded, smacking his leg.

The bell jingled as Mackenzie opened the door. Suddenly, she jerked back, nearly knocking me into the mynah bird's cage. She slammed the door and leaned against it. "Say good-bye to Tony, Barn," she said loudly.

"I did already."

"See if you can make *him* say good-bye." Mackenzie's voice was tight.

Barnaby went over to Tony's cage and looked earnestly up at the bird. "Good-bye," he bellowed. "Good-bye, good-bye—"

"She followed us!" Mackenzie whispered to me. "She's right out there in front of the health-food store."

4

———————●———————

Mackenzie watched out the window till the woman in the purple hat went into the health-food store. Then she snatched Barnaby's hand, ignoring his complaints that Tony still hadn't said good-bye, and we hurried out. When she was sure the woman wasn't watching the street from inside the store, we headed for the corner as fast as we could go.

"Poo-doo doesn't like to run!" Barnaby complained, his short legs churning to keep up with us.

"Of course he does," Mackenzie said. "It's good for him."

The woman hadn't come out of the health-food store

26

before we turned up Clifton Street. Mackenzie breathed a sigh of relief.

We took Barnaby and Poo-doo home, not running anymore but moving fast. The moment his mother opened the front door, Barnaby began telling her about the black gerbils. He didn't even say good-bye as he disappeared inside. But he remembered to hold the door for Poo-doo.

As we walked the three blocks to her house, Mackenzie clutched her tote bag and frowned down at the sidewalk. Obviously, she didn't want to talk. Probably she was concentrating on her feelings. And what could I say, anyway? Except repeat that the old woman showing up all the time was probably coincidence. And there was nothing wrong with wearing weird clothes. Mackenzie, of all people, ought to know that. Anyway, what had the old woman done? Just watched Barnaby.

Still, she *had* come down from the playground to the pond when we did, and then to the square. Maybe she *had* been following us. In spite of myself, I glanced behind me. There's something creepy about the idea that somebody might be following you. The back of my neck got a sort of fizzy feeling.

Maple Park, Ohio, is not a scary place. It's one of a bunch of towns that are sort of jammed together around Cincinnati. They used to be separate, but the city grew out around them. My dad calls it suburban sprawl.

27

We've got houses and condos and apartment buildings and the park and the square and a shopping plaza—not a mall, just a plaza—and churches and schools and a movie theater with four screens. You can ride a bike to anyplace in town in not much more than fifteen minutes. We lock our houses and all that, but for people in Maple Park, crime is mostly something on the news from the city.

But as we walked, I thought of the stories I'd heard about the bad things happening even in unscary places like Maple Park. There was the kid who was riding his bike down the main street in a little town in Minnesota and just disappeared. And the little girl whose mother turned her back for a minute in a big suburban shopping mall and when the mother turned around, the girl was gone.

I glanced back again. The sidewalk was empty and the sun slanted down between the golds and reds of the maple trees. I gave myself a sort of shake. There was nothing evil about the old woman. Just because Mackenzie got a bad feeling didn't mean it was true.

The minute we opened the door and stepped into Mackenzie's front hall, I felt much better. The house was filled, as usual, with wonderful cooking smells. Something spicy and chickeny was the most noticeable.

"Is that you, Mackenzie?" Mrs. Brewster's voice came from the kitchen.

"Who else, Mom?"

"I hoped it was Wanetta. She's bringing the macadamia nuts for the macadamia chicken wings. I needed them half an hour ago."

"Sorry. It's just Casey and me."

"Hi, Casey!" she called. "I'd come out, but I'm up to my elbows in pie dough."

"Hi, Mrs. Brewster. Is that the wings I smell?"

"Except for the macadamias."

"Terrific!" I said.

"They better be terrific! Our whole lives could depend on the party they're for."

"Can Casey stay for supper?" Mackenzie asked.

"If you don't mind wings. They're cheap, so I made extra."

"Great. Anything we can do for you?" I asked, ignoring the look Mackenzie was giving me.

"Thanks, sweetie, but there's nothing to do till Wanetta gets here."

"*Wanetta,*" Mackenzie said, and shook her head as we went up the stairs. She opened the door of her room, flipped the light switch, and went in. I followed, and got the jolt I always get when I go into her room, even though I helped her decorate it. It's all painted indigo. All of it, walls and ceilings and even furniture. Indigo— that's this very deep dark blue. The ceiling is sprinkled with glow-in-the-dark stars, and on the walls are posters of mythical animals and birds and huge flowers. There are blackout shades over the windows, a rainbow

29

comforter on the bed, and a fiber-optic lamp that looks like a glowing sea anemone on the dresser next to a chunk of amethyst crystals.

Last spring, her mom told her she could do anything to her room she wanted, as long as she paid for it and did all the work herself. So she saved her baby-sitting money and the two of us spent one whole weekend painting and putting up posters and sticking stars on the ceiling.

Mrs. Brewster stayed away till we were finished, and when we finally brought her in to see it, I held my breath. I knew what *my* mother would say about a totally indigo room. But Mackenzie's mother just looked at it. "A little dark," she said. "But if you're happy with it, it's okay by me. It's your space."

That's what happens when a mother has a lot of gigantic problems of her own to contend with. I mean, if your husband runs away with a television star and you're suddenly poor and have to start your own business to keep the bills paid, and your only child starts meditating and getting psychic vibrations, what's a little thing like an indigo bedroom?

Mackenzie was searching through the basket of audiotapes next to her bed. "This is my favorite meditation tape," she said, holding one up. "Mayan clay flute music. Gets rid of the mental static really fast. If there are any psychic messages, they come right through." She put it into her tape recorder, settled herself on her bed, and crossed her legs under her. "You want the chair, or would you rather sit on the floor?"

It was obvious she expected me to meditate with her. Sometimes I wished we could go back in time before she got psychic, when the only thing different about Mackenzie was her looks. When we spent our time just talking or messing with our hair or trying out different colors of nail polish. I had two choices. One was to go along with her, close my eyes, sit still till she was finished, and then say I hadn't gotten any messages. The other was to tell her the truth. That I couldn't meditate. That I couldn't even get to the point where I could start listening for psychic messages, since I couldn't get my mind to shut up—or shut down.

When she'd first taught me what I was supposed to do, I'd tried. I really had. I'd focus on my breathing, counting my breaths because that was supposed to concentrate all my thoughts on numbers. But as soon as I started counting, another part of my mind would *think* that I was counting and wonder if I ought to start over. Once, I actually got my mind totally blank for a couple of seconds. I got all excited. It was working. I was doing it. My mind was totally blank! Then I realized that I was *thinking* that my mind was blank. So I'd given up. Now I decided to tell her the truth. Maybe she'd give up on me, too, and let me alone.

When I finished talking, she didn't even blink. She just started sorting through her tapes again. "Harp," she said, holding up another one. "I like harp music for visualization. That's what you can do. When you can't get your mind to go blank, the thing to do is visualize. Instead of stopping your mind, you *use* it."

I sighed. "Okay. What do I do?"

"First, get relaxed, the same way I taught you for meditating. Then, get a picture in your mind. The clearer you can make the picture, the better. Put sound in if you want."

I sat in the straight-backed indigo chair facing her bed. "What kind of picture? What kind of sound?"

Mackenzie changed tapes in the recorder. "Start with the playground. Try to see everything just the way it was, kids and all. Get in as many details as you can. Then put in the woman in the purple hat."

"Then what?"

"Just watch her. Like you're watching a movie. See if you can get any messages, any feelings. Or maybe, while you're watching her, the woman will do something that'll show you what she's up to."

"That's what visualization is for?" I asked. "Getting psychic messages?"

"That's one thing. Some people say you can visualize things you want to happen and they will. But that's not what we need right now. We need to find out anything we can about that woman." She pushed the button and harp music filled the room.

I closed my eyes and took deep breaths. *Visualize*

32

things you want to happen and they will? I thought. Anything you want to happen? Just visualize it and it happens? Anything? It sounded wonderful. Too wonderful. If it really worked, why didn't everybody do it? All the time? About everything?

Then I realized my mind was getting in the way again. I wasn't supposed to be thinking; I was supposed to be relaxing. I concentrated, imagining a warm glow spreading up from my toes, moving through my whole body, up to the top of my head.

I tried to picture the park. It worked. I could see the grass and the trees and the sidewalk. There was the sandbox. The Douglas twins were throwing sand. There were the swings. Barnaby was stomping around, talking to Poo-doo. There was the tree. And the woman in the purple hat. I could see her just standing there, watching Barnaby. I waited to see what she would do. I waited for a feeling. Nothing. I didn't feel anything I hadn't already felt in the park. And she didn't do anything except stand there, watching Barnaby.

It was silly to expect her to do anything I hadn't seen her do, I thought. The pictures were coming from my memory.

I realized I was thinking again.

I tried getting images of the duck pond instead. There were the ducks. The shy one was paddling at the back. I was tossing popcorn. The Douglases were calling, "Duck, duck, duck."

Then, with the harp music filling the room like a waterfall, I must have drifted. I was still at the park, still beside the duck pond. But the kids had faded. So had the ducks.

Jonathan Thayer was coming around the duck pond toward me. His shaggy blond hair was ruffled by a slight breeze. He was smiling that lopsided smile he has. His eyes, piercingly blue, were fixed on me. His backpack hung casually from one shoulder.

I flipped my long, straight ash brown hair over my shoulder and smiled back at him. The sun was warm on my back. A glance in the still water of the pond showed me my reflection. My hair was smooth and shiny. My braces were gone. My nose tilted just slightly up. "Jonathan," I said as he reached my side.

"Casey," he breathed, his voice low and vibrant. He reached out for my hand. I gave it to him. His grip was warm and strong. He raised my hand and brushed his lips lightly across it. "Casey—"

"Well?"

I opened my eyes. The harp music had stopped. Mackenzie was looking at me. It took me a couple of seconds to connect.

"Well?" she asked again, "Did you get any feelings?"

I shook my head. Nothing about the woman in the

34

purple hat, anyway. I didn't think it was a good idea to mention Jonathan Thayer. Still, this visualization stuff was great! Much better than meditation.

"Me, either. At least nothing solid. I kept seeing that purple hat. And now that Barnaby said it, I keep hearing the word *witch,* over and over. I can't seem to get it out of my mind. Do you suppose there's something to it? Do you suppose she could really *be* a witch?"

I laughed. "Don't be silly. Witches aren't real."

"Sure they are. They come on talk shows all the time."

I shook my head. "You've got that word stuck in your mind, that's all. There isn't anything psychic about it." A new smell was wafting into the room. Mrs. Brewster must have put a pie in the oven. If I was going to stay for supper, I had to call home. It was a comforting, ordinary thought. "Listen, Mackenzie, I don't believe these bad feelings you're getting. I think you're just worried about your mom. And the business. You're tired and stressed out and upset."

The doorbell rang downstairs. "Get the door, would you, Mackenzie?" Mrs. Brewster yelled up from the kitchen. "That'll be Wanetta with the macadamia nuts!"

5

————●————

"See? Wanetta's here," I said as we went down to let her in. "The bad feeling you had about her was probably stress, too. So quit worrying."

Mackenzie didn't answer. She just opened the door.

The woman who stood outside the door was enormous. She wasn't fat, just very tall and built like a football player—a scowling bleached-blond football player. She was wearing a gray sweat suit, and had a jar of macadamia nuts in each huge hand. "Hi, Wanetta," Mackenzie said.

The woman stormed through the door, brushing Mackenzie and me out of the way like gnats. "Eight dollars and ninety-five cents!" she boomed. "For four ounces! What do they think this stuff is, gold? It's a crime, that's what it is. A crime!" The chandelier above us seemed to sway from the force of her voice.

Mackenzie's mother appeared in the doorway to the kitchen. She was wiping her hands on the Unicorn Catering apron she wore over her turtleneck and blue jeans. Wisps of graying chestnut hair had pulled loose from her hair clip and straggled around her damp forehead. I've always thought of Mrs. Brewster as tall, but Wanetta dwarfed her. She looked up into the woman's broad pink face. "What is it, Wanetta? What's the matter?"

Wanetta held up the jars like evidence in a courtroom. "Eight dollars and ninety-five cents for four ounces of fat little nuts. That's nearly thirty-six dollars a pound!"

I was impressed with the speed of her mental math calculations. Also, with the cost of the macadamia nuts.

"How can people eat nuts that cost thirty-six dollars a pound?"

Mrs. Brewster smiled uncertainly. "I guess if they really like them—"

"Yeah, well there are lots of people who really like meat, too. And milk for their kids. But they can't afford 'em."

Mrs. Brewster shrugged. "I'm sure that's true, Wanetta, and I'm sorry about that. But the Freidels asked me to fix macadamia chicken wings for their party, and I don't see how—"

"I've been thinking all the way here from the store. I thought I'd like this job, getting to see how the other half lives and all. But this"—she brandished the nut jars in the air—"this is too much."

Mrs. Brewster rescued the jars and clutched them to her apron.

"How the other half lives is criminal, that's what it is," Wanetta went on. "They use stuff just for flavoring that costs more than other folks have to feed a whole family a whole day. It's wrong. Just plain wrong. Nothing against you, Mrs. B., but I gotta quit this job." Mackenzie gave me a look.

Mrs. Brewster's face had gone white. She opened her mouth and closed it again. Opened it and closed it. But no sound came out.

Mackenzie spoke up. "Wanetta, there are lots of rich people in the world. Nothing you can do will change that. If Unicorn Catering doesn't make them their macadamia chicken wings, somebody else will."

Wanetta folded her arms across her chest. "That's as may be. But I can't do it anymore. Not with so many people homeless."

Mrs. Brewster was holding on to the macadamia nuts as if they were life rings and she'd just been thrown overboard. "You'll stay and do this party, won't you? This *very important party?*"

"Can't. It's a question of right and wrong."

"Tell you what," Mrs. Brewster said. "You stay on and I'll give you a bonus every time anybody orders macadamia chicken wings. You can give the bonus to the homeless!"

Wanetta shook her head. "It ain't just the nuts. It was starting to bother me even before. I can't go on cooking and serving expensive food to folks who don't eat half of it, they're so busy drinking and gabbing about their fancy cars and their fancy houses and their fancy jobs. I couldn't hold up my head in front of my kids. I'll go back to working at my cousin Buddy's diner."

"But you said he didn't pay enough—"

"I'll just work more hours. Sometimes you gotta stand up for your principles. Even if it's hard. There's more to life than money."

Mackenzie's mother looked at the chandelier, the walls, the stairs. "Maybe so, Wanetta, but it doesn't pay the mortgage."

Wanetta patted her shoulder. "I don't blame you, Mrs. B. You gotta do what you gotta do. But so do I. Just mail me my check." She went to the door. "Good luck!" The door thundered shut behind her and Mrs. Brewster burst into tears.

I looked at Mackenzie and she looked at me. Another bad feeling come true.

39

When Mrs. Brewster stopped crying, Mackenzie offered the two of us as servers for the party Saturday night.

My parents don't do a lot of entertaining. All they do is invite a couple of friends over sometimes for spaghetti-and-video parties. I'd never been to a formal grown-up party before. I chewed on my fingernails all the way to the Freidels' Saturday night, in the Brewsters' Voyager filled with pots and bowls and trays covered with plastic.

Mrs. Brewster was explaining why this party was so important. The Freidels were very, very rich and knew just about everybody who was anybody. All the people who would be at their house that night gave a lot of parties of their own. If the Freidels' guests liked the food, they would probably want Unicorn Catering to do their parties, too. It was the biggest job Mrs. Brewster had had since she quit specializing in desserts. Most of the recipes were new, and this was a test of what she called her "new profile."

"I'm trying gourmet touches to normal dishes—macadamia wings, saffron dip, anchovy-prosciutto-cheese puffs. This isn't a dinner, just a cocktail party. They're all going on to a black-tie charity benefit afterward."

And I, dressed in my black velvet dress with the white lace collar, was going to be serving. It was worse than facing Jonathan Thayer and a math exam at the same time. What if I dropped a tray of chicken wings on some lady's silk skirt? Or bumped into somebody and spilled their champagne?

"Just visualize the party and you doing everything perfectly," Mackenzie told me as I tore my thumbnail practically off. "You'll be fine."

Easy for her to say. She looked spectacular in a black skirt and a white satin blouse of her mother's, with her long hair piled up on her head. No matter what she did, everybody would think she was wonderful. They'd probably want to hire Unicorn Catering just so she'd come and serve.

While the van bounced along, I tried visualizing. But it isn't easy to visualize something you've never seen before. I had to make everything up. And then when we got there, nothing was the way I'd expected it to be. First of all, the house was much bigger, hardly like a house at all. It was made of stone, with huge windows of little diamond-shaped panes of glass with lead around them, all lighted up with floodlights, and about the size of Maple Park Middle School. We drove around to the back, where there was a two-story carriage house with a matching pair of BMW's inside.

I was expecting people about the age of my grandparents—people who'd had a whole lifetime to make their fortune. But the harried-looking woman who met us at the back door looked younger than my mom or Mrs.

Brewster. She had blond hair, cut very short, and she was wearing a long, tight dress all covered with black sequins. She was in her stocking feet, though, and trying to close the catch on a jeweled bracelet.

She was surprised to see Mackenzie and me, but Mrs. Brewster explained that her assistant had come down with the flu. "I wouldn't have wanted to leave you in the lurch," she said, and Mrs. Freidel just nodded in a distracted way and had her fasten the bracelet. Then she went off to see if the bartenders had everything they needed.

"Bartenders?" I asked.

"You don't think people like this pour drinks for their guests with their own little hands," Mrs. Brewster said.

Once the guests arrived, there wasn't much time to be scared. I had to concentrate on carrying the hors d'oeuvre trays without tipping them, making my way between the elbows of women in silk and velvet and sequins and beads, and the men in black tuxedos, all of whom had drinks in their hands. Mackenzie just sort of floated around with her tray, weaving in and out as if she'd been doing this all her life. I could see all the men noticing her. Nobody noticed me until I put my tray practically in their faces. "Macadamia wings?" I'd say, the way Mrs. Brewster had taught me.

Like the Freidels, the guests were much younger than I'd expected. Wanetta wasn't entirely right about what people at such a party talk about. I didn't hear much about fancy houses and cars. There was a lot of talk about jobs, though. It seemed as if everybody there, men and women, had some high-powered job that kept them very busy and involved a lot of stress.

Another thing most of them talked about was kids. If they had them, they talked about day care or private school or trying to find a nanny. If they didn't, they talked about whether they should, or why they didn't, or how long they had to decide.

The other popular topic was fitness. It seemed as if every single person there, from the tall, thin lady in the red silk jumpsuit to the dumpy little man with the big mustache and the funny-looking toupee, was into running. Or walking. Or biking or aerobics or weight training. So they talked about health clubs and Lycra tights and Italian racing bikes and running shoes.

Things were going fine until about halfway through the evening when somebody mentioned cholesterol. I was there when it started. A teeny woman with a waist about the size of my wrist asked the dumpy man what his cholesterol count was. When he answered, she shrieked and actually snatched away the chicken wing he'd just taken off my tray. "Are you trying to kill yourself?" she asked him, waving the wing under his nose. "This still has skin on it! Do you *know* how much fat there is under the skin of a chicken? This thing's as deadly as a Big Mac!"

"But it's a party!" he said.

"You think that makes a difference to your heart?"

Before you could say *macadamia,* everybody was talking about fat and cholesterol and comparing their cholesterol counts. There didn't seem to be anyone there who didn't know what theirs was. And suddenly, nobody was taking wings anymore. You'd have thought I was carrying a tray full of rat poison for all the business I was getting.

"Three hundred and thirty?" I heard someone say. "And you're eating a *cheese* puff? Do you want to drop dead on the tennis court at forty-five?" Now people began moving away from the buffet table.

Mackenzie had just brought in a tray of fresh vegetables, and she was mobbed. Someone asked her what was in the dip, and she had the good sense to say yogurt. She didn't mention the sour cream. I made two more trips around the room, with nobody taking a single chicken wing, and then a guy with a red paisley cummerbund came swooping down on me and took five wings—almost all I had left—and stacked them on his plate. "One hundred and ten!" he announced, holding his plate up where everyone could see. "My cholesterol count is one hundred and ten. I can *live* on butter and salami—and wings. Bring on the prime rib!" People actually booed.

Eventually, after a lot of talk about arteries and heart attacks and CPR and blood pressure, someone mentioned a local congressman who was being investigated for tax evasion and the conversation changed. But almost the only things that got eaten after that were the fruits and vegetables. I noticed that the dips went, too. I guess even fitness freaks don't much like plain broccoli.

When it was all over, and we were in the kitchen cleaning up, Mrs. Freidel came in, still looking harried. "Where would you like us to put the leftovers?" Mackenzie's mom asked, motioning to the trays of pastries and cheese puffs and wings.

"Take them with you," Mrs. Freidel said. "Just take everything with you! I never want to see a chicken wing again!"

"After tonight, I'll be known as the Ptomaine Mary of catering," Mrs. Brewster said when Mrs. Freidel had left for the dinner. "They probably think I'm out to kill off the entire wealthy population of Ohio." She held up the china boxful of Unicorn Catering business cards that she'd put out on the buffet table. "I don't think a single person took one of these. None of them will want me to do their parties."

"You didn't tell Mrs. Freidel what to order," Mackenzie reminded her. "You just gave her the choices."

"Right. Choices like deadly chicken wings and cheese puffs! All they care about is their arteries. What do they expect at a party, alfalfa sprouts and fish oil?" She tucked plastic wrap over a tray of leftover wings. "I

45

know you should take the skin off chicken when you cook it! But if you take the skin off wings, there's nothing left. And they were good!"

"They were great, Mom," Mackenzie said, putting cheese puffs into a plastic container. "We'll have them for dinner the rest of the week. Think of the money that'll save."

Mrs. Brewster was not comforted.

"I might as well just quit," she said later as we drove home. "First people don't want my desserts. Then, when I find some great gourmet recipes and expand my offerings, they don't want those, either. What am I going to do for a profile? I can't make a living on broccoli and yogurt dip. It might be good for people, but they don't really *want* it!" She turned on the radio. Jazz music filled the van. "Whatever made me think I could run a business?" she asked.

"You'll think of something," Mackenzie said. "You're a terrific cook, Mom. All you need is some new recipes—low-cholesterol ones."

"Mmmmmph," her mother said. "What I need is food stamps. Or maybe I could go work for Wanetta's cousin Buddy."

We rode a while listening to the music. I was exhausted. Serving's a lot tougher than you'd think.

"Visualize!" Mackenzie whispered as I was almost nodding off to sleep among the leftovers. "Picture new recipes. Lots of business. Success. Nobody's going to get the Brewster women down! If you visualize something often enough, it can happen. Let's do it."

"Okay." But when I tried to get a picture of a success-ful party, all I could see was my own soft, wonderful bed.

6

By the time church was over that rainy Sunday, I had put Unicorn Catering's problems out of my mind. It was time to face my own. I tackled the algebra homework that was due Monday. Catastrophe! As I looked at the numbers and letters on the page, several other words came into my mind—*calamity, cataclysm, disaster,* and *fiasco.* I listened to my subliminal tape. It put me to sleep. I tried visualizing getting all the problems right. As I was trying to concentrate on seeing a big red *A* on my paper, Jonathan Thayer appeared in my visualization and that was the end of algebra. I gave up.

"Help!" I begged Ian, who was, as usual, on the phone.

He covered the receiver. "Sorry, dunce. Shannon and I are going bowling. You're going to have to handle this one on your own."

Dunce, he'd called me. I'd have kicked him, but he was right. I *couldn't* do it on my own. "How about after?"

"I'm taking Wendy to the movies."

I sat in my room, staring blankly at my wall—my posters, my books. And got an idea. I had plenty of books about words—three different dictionaries, a thesaurus, and some about the origins of words. Maybe there were books about numbers, too. I didn't have any, of course, but the library might—*Algebra Made Easy* or *Higher Math for Dunces* or something like that.

I put on my slicker and went, tromping through puddles and soaking my feet. The minute I got inside the big double doors, I felt better. The Maple Park Library is one of my favorite places. I like the smell— dust, books, furniture polish. And I love research. In the main room, there is the huge card catalog with its neat, long SUBJECT/TITLE drawers. I like pulling them out to look for books, and using one of those little yellow pencils to write down their titles and call numbers on the slips of paper the library keeps at the catalog table. It makes me feel grown-up and organized. In control.

Maybe because of the rain, it was a busy day at the library. At least one person was sitting at nearly every table. There were a couple of girls from my English class working on a paper I'd already finished. And Howie Mankowitz, surrounded by big dusty-looking books, was sitting at a table next to the only empty one. He looked up and grinned when I put my bookbag on the empty table and hung my slicker on a chair. "History paper," he said, pointing at his books.

I nodded. I didn't tell him what I was there for. It made me feel like a fool; *he* certainly didn't need any extra help in math. He was Mrs. Mendez's star.

Then I went to the card catalog. And for the first time in my life, the library let me down. The closest thing I could find to what I wanted was one from the children's room called *I Hate Mathematics*. I agreed with the title, but the book itself didn't help me any.

I had decided just to escape into a good mystery when Mackenzie showed up. She plopped down at the table with me and right away it seemed that Howie Mankowitz was losing interest in his history paper. He kept looking over at us.

"What are you here for?" I asked. Mackenzie doesn't share my love of research.

"Mom sent me to find new recipes," she said. "You want to help?"

I considered for about ten seconds. It would be much more fun than the impossible task that was waiting for me at home. "Sure. What kind does she want?"

Mackenzie shrugged. "I think she's gone a little overboard about the reaction last night. She's decided her new profile should be health foods. Not just *healthy* foods—the real hard-core stuff.''

"You mean vegetarian dishes?"

"No. She has some gourmet vegetarian cookbooks at home, and she says they're all full of cheese and cream—high-cholesterol evil stuff. She wants real health foods—sprouts. Tofu. Like that."

"Yuck. She thinks people want that at parties?"

"After last night, she doesn't want anybody ever to accuse her of making unhealthy food again. She says if healthy food is what they want, that's exactly what she'll give them. She'll just have to find some way to make it taste good."

"Okay. You look under health foods, I'll try cholesterol, and 'Low,' for low fat, low sugar . . ."

"Low everything," she said.

This was more like it. In a few minutes, I had plenty of titles and numbers written down. Our library may not be much on books about math, but it has millions of cookbooks. Most of the call numbers were close together, so I just went to the shelves and started looking. It's amazing. No matter what you want to cook, somebody has written a book about it. There were three just about chocolate! There were books about southern cooking and Amish cooking, pasta, cheese, salads, high carbohydrates, low salt, deep-fried, and way over in one corner two about cooking weeds you find along the side of the road. And plenty about health foods.

In no time, I had a stack I could barely carry with my chin on top to hold them. I lugged them to the table and spread them out. A few minutes later, as I was separating the low-calorie books from the low-sodium ones, the low-sugar from the low-fats, Mackenzie came and plopped down four books.

"Four?" I whispered. "That's all you could find?" I waved at the books taking up the table in front of me. "Guess I got all the rest."

On the top of Mackenzie's little stack was one called *Macrobiotics for the New Age.* I'd seen that but passed it up because it sounded more like medicine than party food. Then I noticed the title of the next one—*Witchcraft Through the Ages.* Under that was *A History of Witches,* and *Witchcraft in the Modern World.* I just looked at her.

"Listen, Casey," she said, "I've been thinking about the bad luck Mom's been having. What if it isn't luck?"

"What do you mean?"

"What if it's a curse of some kind? A spell?"

"Mackenzie! You're not still thinking about that old woman." Howie looked over at us, and I lowered my voice. "That's ridiculous."

She shook her head. "It's not! Most of these books have a whole section about curses."

"Even if there were such a thing, why would anybody, especially some old lady you don't even know, want to put a curse on your mother's business?"

"I don't know. For practice maybe. Anyway, it can't hurt to find out about witches, Case. This one was written by someone who says she *is* one! I read the jacket flap, and she says there are lots of witches around; it's like a religion. They have regular meetings and everything. The least we can do is read about them." She handed me *Witchcraft Through the Ages*.

I glanced at the cookbooks. Even if I didn't believe in witches and curses for a minute, I had to admit they were more interesting than low-fat recipes. I opened the book. She was right, after all. Finding out about witches couldn't hurt.

A few minutes later, I wasn't so sure. I was getting a sick feeling in my stomach. "The witch hies herself to dark and empty places," I read, "to tombs and ruins; for her sacrifices of animals and humans must not be known." Sacrifices? Human sacrifices? I could feel goose bumps rising on my arms, even right there in the middle of the library. My image of witches had been all about black hats and nose warts and broomsticks. I didn't know they went in for human sacrifices. I was about to tell Mackenzie about the human sacrifices when she leaned over to me.

"It says here they use spells to turn nature's forces against their enemies. They can talk to animals and change shapes—"

"You don't believe that!"

"And raise the dead. Sometimes"—Mackenzie's voice got very low and I had to lean closer to hear her—"sometimes they *eat human flesh.*"

"Mackenzie!" I accidentally said that so loud that Howie Mankowitz jumped and even the librarian, who was clear across at the main desk, looked up and shook her head at me. "That's enough!" I whispered. "I don't want to know another thing about witches. Anyway, it's all just stories. People can't change their shapes or raise the dead or any of that. There aren't any real witches." I closed the book in front of me and shoved it toward her. "And even if some people *say* they are, they're probably just nuts who want to believe they've got special powers."

Mackenzie pointed to an old-fashioned engraving in her book. It showed a man in a dungeonlike place, reading from a gigantic book and holding a bowlful of liquid from a steaming cauldron. On the floor near his feet was the body of a little boy—a boy who looked just about Barnaby's age. "She's been watching Barnaby, Case. It says sometimes they use babies or children to work their spells."

The feeling in my stomach was getting worse. "That picture is only meant to scare people. Anyway, be sensible. People wouldn't *admit* they were witches if that meant they went around killing little kids."

Mackenzie closed her book. "There are two kinds of magic—white and black. The ones who go on television probably just work white magic. Or just *talk* about that kind."

"Put the witch books back," I said, "and we'll take these cookbooks to your mom." For once, Mackenzie did what I said instead of the other way around.

The librarian gave us plastic bags for the books, because it was still raining when we left. Even under my slicker hood, I could feel my hair frizzing up with every step I took.

"If there *were* spells, I'd want one to make the rain quit," I said.

"Spells are dangerous if you aren't really a witch," Mackenzie said. "That book said you could die if you got a word wrong in a spell or one wrong ingredient in a potion."

"Mackenzie, I was kidding!"

"I know. But I'm not. You said my feeling about Wanetta was just stress. But it was right. And the other bad feeling is still there. If anything, it's worse. What if she's after Barnaby to make her spells more powerful? It's my job to take care of him. I'm going to keep Barnaby at his house or mine for a while—away from anyplace the woman in the purple hat might be."

"Okay. All right. Now, no more talk about witches. It makes my stomach hurt."

It was good to get to the Brewsters'. The smell of warm chocolate chased any thoughts about witches and black magic away.

55

"Just in time," Mrs. Brewster called from the kitchen when we dropped our wet bags full of books onto the floor. "Come have some high-cholesterol, high-fat, high-calorie, sugar-filled chocolate fudge brownies!"

"We've come to save the day," Mackenzie said as we went into the cozy red and white kitchen where her mother was pulling a pan out of the oven. "We've got hundreds of recipes for the New Age Health Food Unicorn Catering."

"Full of oat bran and fish oil?" Mrs. Brewster asked, setting the pan on the table.

"Oat bran and tofu," Mackenzie said.

"And brown rice," I added, remembering the book I'd found that used brown rice in every recipe.

"Sounds delicious!"

"And we'll help you start trying them out," Mackenzie promised. *"After* brownies."

Mrs. Brewster opened the freezer. "Brownies and ice cream," she said. "I went down to Graeter's and got double chocolate chip. Comfort food now, health food later."

7

In the next few days, I spent some of my time doing regular stuff—hanging around where Jonathan Thayer might show up, listening to ocean waves, and paying attention for half an hour every night while Ian tried to explain problems that had trains coming at each other. But it seemed as if I spent lots more worrying about Mackenzie and her mother—and Unicorn Catering.

Mrs. Brewster hadn't been able to find a new assistant yet. Two girls answered her ad in the paper. One, who said she had graduated from high school, couldn't read well enough to follow a recipe. The second one showed up in raggedy jeans with a mohawk haircut tipped with orange, four nose studs, and about ten earrings. I couldn't imagine people like the Freidels letting her inside their house, but Mrs. Brewster was almost desperate enough to take a chance on her, until she said she had to get paid ten dollars an hour. Mrs. Brewster just laughed. So Mackenzie and I—along with Barnaby—went to help after school every day.

Mackenzie didn't have to worry about keeping Barnaby away from the woman in the purple hat. She wasn't likely to show up in their kitchen. And we were so busy that the subject of witches got shoved clear to the backs of our minds—mine, anyway.

We found things for Barnaby to do in the kitchen while we tried the health-food recipes. Sometimes there were jobs he could do to help, like washing vegetables or sorting dried beans. Mrs. Brewster named us the Unicorn Catering Auxiliary Task Force. Barnaby wanted a uniform, so Mackenzie made an ATF arm band and sewed a unicorn patch on a baseball hat for him. He wanted a hat for Poo-doo, too, but Mackenzie told him the Auxiliary Canine Corps didn't wear hats.

Mrs. Brewster threw herself into the health-food business with everything she had. She bought tofu. She bought beans and lentils and a bunch of stuff I'd never heard of before called kasha, bulgur wheat, tempeh, tahini, and miso. And then, because one of the books said it was absolutely necessary for proper nutrition, she bought seaweed. Seaweed! Two kinds.

That week we all—even Barnaby *and* Poo-doo—tasted Deviled Tofu, Tofu Lasagna, Tofu à L'Orange, and Spicy Tofu and Eggplant in Black Bean Sauce. Except for the last one—he spit out the eggplant—Barnaby liked them all. Mackenzie and I did not. Mrs. Brewster smiled a lot when she tasted each recipe. After all, she'd put a lot of time and effort, not to say money, into making them. And coming up with recipes that tasted terrific was really important to her. But I could tell by her eyes—and the fact that she shared a lot of her servings with Barnaby—that she didn't like them any better than we did.

Boiled Green Salad with Sprouts gave me a chance to use one of my favorite words—*execrable!* We tried Kasha with Vegetable Gravy, Tempeh Stew, and Millet-Vegetable Casserole. Even Barnaby didn't like any of those. A couple of times, Mackenzie and I hinted that maybe this wasn't such a useful profile for Unicorn Catering, but Mrs. Brewster wasn't listening. The Freidels' party had made health food an obsession.

Thursday afternoon, we got to the cookbook that said you couldn't be healthy without seaweed. So we tried it. Both kinds came dried and had to be soaked. Barnaby liked that part. The kind called *wakame* turned from black sticks into great big slimy green leaves. "Magic!" Barnaby said as Mrs. Brewster fished one of the leaves out of the soaking water.

"It smells like the beach," Mrs. Brewster said. "Like shells and sand and"—she made a face—"dead horseshoe crabs."

The kind called *arame* is sort of pretty when it's dry—crispy fronds, very delicate and light. But when it's soaked, it turns into long greenish black strings—like a bird nest that's been through a hurricane.

We put the first kind into soup—cut up in "bite-sized pieces"—and cooked the second kind with carrots and onions. Barnaby took one taste of each and put them on the floor for Poo-doo. "Poo-doo likes seaweed," he said. "Poo-doo *needs* seaweed."

That whole cookbook went into the reject pile.

When we got to the house after school Friday, Mrs. Brewster was frazzled. She had a Businesswomen's Club buffet dinner that night, and she'd promised them a delicious health-food main dish (the new profile had apparently worked for the businesswomen) along with the usual hors d'oeuvres, raw veggies and dip, and a chocolate fondue with fresh fruit. She figured that was as healthy as a dessert ought to get. The only main-dish recipe we'd tried that came close to being edible, let alone delicious, was Tofu Lasagna. She had hired somebody from a temporary-services company to help her serve, and everything except the lasagna was ready. She had the sauce on the stove and the noodles all cooked, but she didn't have enough tofu.

60

"Could you kids run down to the square and get me a couple more pounds?" she asked. "It's a task-force supply mission."

"Hurray, hurray!" said Barnaby. Partly he liked tofu and partly he was desperate to get outdoors for a change.

The health-food store, called Over the Rainbow, has been on the square for a long time—five or six years at least. But I'd never been inside before. When we went in, Barnaby telling Poo-doo that we couldn't go next door to visit the gerbils because we were "on a mission," the first thing we saw were huge bins full of grains and beans. Next to us on the right wall were shelves full of books. I checked a couple of titles—*Tissue Cleansing Through Bowel Management* and *Planetary Herbology,* not exactly light reading. I wondered who shopped here. On the left wall under a hand-lettered sign that said HERBS AND SPICES were shelves of glass jars and bottles full of different colored powders and crushed leaves.

Mackenzie went to the coolers at the back of the store for the tofu and Barnaby headed for a rack of candy and cookies. It was next to the counter, where a guy with a ponytail was sitting on a high stool, so I figured Barnaby was okay on his own.

I went to look at the labels on the herb jars. Mugwart, pennyroyal, myrrh gum, burdock root, juniper berries,

61

and red clover. Whatever happened to garlic and oregano and cinnamon and ginger? And what were all these weird things used for? I imagined Mrs. Brewster trying to sell a client on a dinner of turkey and mugwart, with juniper berries for dessert. Then the subject of witches pushed back up to the front of my brain. It seemed to me I'd seen names like some of these in the book on witchcraft.

I shook the thought away and went into the aisles, looking at the bags and boxes and jars on the shelves. There were all sorts of weird things, from cashew butter to walnut oil and peppermint soap with glycerine. Then I saw a swivel rack like the ones at convenience stores that hold potato chips and pretzels and popcorn. I went to see if there was something normal there I could get the three of us for munchies on the walk home.

The first bags I checked turned out to be pasta. But these weren't just ordinary noodles. There was raspberry pasta and basil pasta. Then I found squid ink pasta. Mackenzie was coming back from the cooler, carrying two packages of tofu. "I couldn't decide which kind," she said.

"Never mind the tofu." I held up the bag. "Take a look at this—it's *squid ink pasta.*"

"It's what?"

"Looking's okay, kid," we heard from the front. "But no touching, okay?"

"Come back here with us, Barn," Mackenzie called as she took the package of pale purple noodles from me. "I wonder what squid ink's supposed to be good for. Do people really eat this stuff?"

Barnaby came around the rack, holding up a candy bar. "Can I have this, 'Kenzie?"

She looked at it. "You know what this is, Barn?"

"Candy," he said.

"It's called tofu chocolate."

I had just taken off the rack a bag of corn chips that looked just like regular corn chips, except they were navy blue—when the door opened and someone else came in. We were behind the rack and couldn't see up to the front of the store, but I caught a glimpse of the purple hat.

"Shhhh," Mackenzie said to Barnaby, who was starting to tell Poo-doo about tofu chocolate. He shushed. Maybe it was the look on her face. It got to me, too. In spite of myself, I felt goose bumps rise along my arms.

"Hello, Ms.—" the clerk said. "And what'll it be for you today?" He had said a name, but I hadn't gotten it.

"Hello, Greg. Would you believe I'm clear out of parsley? Better give me eight ounces this time. I've been using an awful lot lately."

The woman's voice sounded very ordinary. No cackles. No witchy sound. And she was ordering parsley. Plain, ordinary parsley.

Barnaby held up his candy bar. "Can I—" he started.

Mackenzie put her hand over his mouth. "This is a *secret* mission," she whispered.

The woman was speaking to the clerk again. "An ounce of comfrey, some genseng, henbane, a little moonwort—"

Mackenzie set down the tofu, took a pen and a scrap of paper out of her bag, and began writing furiously.

"And most important of all," the woman said, "devil's claw root. Give me the large bottle, please."

"Devil's claw root?" I whispered.

Mackenzie looked at me. "What did I tell you? She *is* a witch!"

8

———————•———————

When the clerk had bagged all her purchases, the woman said, "Put it on my tab, Greg," and left. She hadn't seen us.

"Did the witch go away?" Barnaby asked, his eyes big.

"Witch?" Mackenzie said, her voice all high and squeaky. "What do you mean witch?"

"You said she was a—"

"No, no. *Rich*. That woman is very *rich*. There aren't any real witches, Barn. Didn't I tell you that? Let's go pay for our things."

"Okay." Barnaby accepted the change of subject

without a fuss. He had more important things on his mind. "I'm getting tofu chocolate!"

While the man rang up our stuff, I thought about witches. I didn't believe in them. But then I hadn't believed in psychic messages before Mackenzie started getting them, either. If those could be real—and I knew now that they could—what other weird things might be real? Devil's claw root, she had ordered. What was it? What was it for? I told myself the whole thing was silly. I wasn't afraid of an old woman just because she dressed strangely and bought weird herbs.

But what about Mackenzie's feeling? I found myself glancing around when we left the store, just to be sure the woman wasn't out there anywhere.

Mackenzie did the same, I noticed. And all the way home, she had a sort of haunted look in her eyes. She held Barnaby's hand as if she was afraid somebody was going to snatch him away right there on the street. Whatever she'd told Barnaby, Mackenzie didn't have any doubts at all, I could tell. As far as she was concerned, the woman in the purple hat was a witch.

To get her mind—and mine—off the old woman, I opened up my very expensive bag of blue corn chips. They turned out to be good—just like any other corn chips, except for the color. The bag said they were made from organically grown Native American blue corn, lightly salted with sea salt, and fried in oil high in "beneficial mono-unsaturates." It was nice to be eating

66

something that tasted just like junk food but was really good for you.

Barnaby gave each of us one square of his tofu chocolate. It tasted exactly like a Hershey bar. He was actually disappointed that it wasn't anything at all like tofu. But he was crazy about the blue chips. By the time we were halfway back to Mackenzie's, the three of us (and Poo-doo, of course—Barnaby kept taking extra chips for Poo-doo) had demolished the whole bag.

At the Brewsters', we took Barnaby and Poo-doo into the fenced-in backyard to play on Mackenzie's old swing set while the Tofu Lasagna was baking. We sat on the back steps and watched him. For a long time, neither of us said anything. But I was pretty sure we were both thinking about the same thing.

"I'm scared," Mackenzie said finally. "And I don't want Barnaby to know it. We mustn't mention witches around him again. It could traumatize him. He's so sensitive—"

I looked at Barnaby, who had jumped off the swing and was stomping on ants, shouting, "Gotcha!" with every stomp.

"We've got to *do* something," she said. "I don't know what yet, but something. Maybe we could report her to the police."

I could just imagine tromping into the police station to report that there was a witch loose in Maple Park. "They'd laugh us out the door."

She thought for a minute, then nodded. "You're probably right. But there must be something—"

Barnaby called to her from the top of the slide to watch him go down on his tummy, and we didn't mention the subject again.

But it didn't go away. That night, I had a nightmare. I was serving at the Freidels' party again and Mrs. Brewster had sent me out with a whole trayful of seaweed. Nobody would take any. I kept offering and offering, and everybody kept saying no and making these awful faces. I had a terrible feeling I was letting Mackenzie and her mother down, ruining Unicorn Catering.

Finally, the woman in the red silk jumpsuit said she'd take some. But when she reached out her hand, it wasn't a hand at all; on the end of her arm was a huge red devil's claw. She started to laugh a horrible cackling laugh and when I looked up at her, she had turned into an old, old woman wearing a pointed witch's hat—a purple one. She started to reach for me with that gigantic claw, but Mackenzie was there suddenly, and the woman got her instead. As she started to drag Mackenzie away, I woke up to an ordinary Saturday morning.

I'd had enough of feelings and suspicions and doubts once and for all. What I needed was real, solid information, something to prove there was nothing to worry about. Since I wasn't psychic, I was going to have to rely on more ordinary ways of finding it. Right after breakfast, I called Mackenzie. "On your way to Barnaby's this morning, would you bring me that list you made of what the woman in the purple hat ordered at the store yesterday?"

"I don't know if it'll do any good," she said. "I meditated on it last night and didn't get anything new."

"Just bring it," I said. And she did.

When the library opened, I was waiting on the steps, Mackenzie's notes in one hand, my notebook and pen in the other. I gathered every single book I could find that had anything to do with witches or herbs and settled in.

There were basically two kinds of witch books. One kind had information about witches that seemed to come mostly from the confessions of witches who were about to get burned at the stake. The one I had read before was one of those. The information didn't seem to me to be very reliable, once I thought about it. All that stuff about pacts with the devil and casting spells and doing black magic seemed to be just what the people who were going to burn them expected them to say. Maybe they said what everybody wanted to hear in hopes of getting off.

The other kind of book was about modern witches. The one Mackenzie had found that was written by a real witch said that witches don't worship the devil or make pacts with him. In fact, it said that most of them don't even believe in the devil. They believe in nature and try to work with it and use its power for their own purposes.

They use herbs for healing and for making spells. And they can do curses, though the author said most of them would only do a curse to punish somebody evil, not just to be mean—*malicious* was the word she used. I didn't like finding out that witches even *think* they can work curses. That wasn't going to make Mackenzie feel any better. At least none of these books talked about killing children. I looked in two other books about modern witches. They didn't agree about witches using spells only for good, but they did say witches could cast them. This was not what I'd wanted to find. And I didn't like it that all the books didn't agree. How was I supposed to know which ones to believe?

I had just opened a book about voodoo that had a whole chapter on curses when Howie Mankowitz plopped a bunch of books down on the other end of my table and sat down. He smiled, and I smiled back. His smile was kind of nice, I noticed. But he was definitely no Jonathan Thayer. I went back to reading about voodoo witch doctors.

This book, at least, was supposed to be completely based on scientific studies. I took out my pen to make notes. But it was worse than the others. It said that when people believe in curses, the curses actually work. In parts of the world where people believe in voodoo, if a person knows he's been cursed, he dies—

just dies. He doesn't have to be sick first or anything. All it takes to make the curse work is believing it will. That proves how much power the mind has over the body, the book said.

I got chills all up and down my back reading that. If Mackenzie really believed she was cursed, then it didn't matter whether she really was or not. I needed to show her *proof* that she wasn't.

I shoved the witch books out of my way and started on the ones about herbs. Maybe I could show Mackenzie that everything the woman had bought was just as innocent and ordinary as parsley—even devil's claw root. The trouble was, every single herb book, even the big innocent-looking one with the color pictures, called *The Complete Book of Herbs and Spices,* talked perfectly casually about witches. It had a whole chapter on poisonous herbs that started with a paragraph about witches' brews, spells, and curses.

One of the herbs in that chapter was henbane. I looked at Mackenzie's notes. There it was—henbane. The woman had bought some. Henbane, the book said, was a poison, related to deadly nightshade, sometimes used as a sedative.

I looked for devil's claw root in the index, but there wasn't any listing. In another book, one just about roots, I found devil's bit, devil's bones, and devil's ear, but no devil's claw.

In all the herb books, there were explanations of

what various herbs were supposed to do. Some were for healing, some for eating, some for poisoning people or casting spells. The comfrey the woman had ordered was good for reducing the swelling around broken bones; the ginseng was supposed to be good for just about everything. It was called a "restorative tonic." I was losing track of which things were supposed to be scientifically proven and which were just reports of old beliefs.

Then I opened a small book called *A Witch's Guide to Gardening,* which told what a witch ought to grow in her garden. I was just flipping through it when I came to a full-page drawing of a parsley plant. The caption said that parsley was one of the most magical—and evil—plants of all. Parsley, according to the text, used to be called "devil's oatmeal." All of a sudden, it seemed as if the lights in the library dimmed. Shadows seemed to be reaching across the table at me. I remembered what the woman had said when she ordered her parsley—"I've been using an awful lot lately."

I looked up and found Howie Mankowitz staring at me. Had I said something out loud? I tried to smile casually, then turned back to the books. One of them had a chapter on protection against black magic. I flipped open the notebook I'd brought and started making notes as fast as I could.

9

———●———

Mackenzie would be at Barnaby's house, I was pretty sure, so that's where I went when I left the library. I was thinking about witches. And spells. And curses. There was a bright blue sky overhead, the sun was warm, and the leaves were all red and orange. But I barely noticed. It was October; in a couple of weeks it would be Halloween. I wasn't sure I'd ever feel the same way about seeing little kids running around in witch costumes.

One of the books had said that lots of modern medicines came from herbal cures that had first been used by witches. So the herbs could be good. But they were also poisonous and some of the medicines made from them even today could kill people if used the wrong way. Henbane, the book had said, was one of the deadliest herbs, along with nightshade and wolfbane, hemlock and mandrake. The woman had ordered henbane. *Henbane, nightshade, wolfbane, hemlock.* The words began to sound evil all by themselves.

I clutched my notebook to my chest as I walked. I didn't really need the notes inside. The protections from witchcraft were fennel, carraway, and the color red. I started saying them over and over, as if they were a spell to drive out those other words. *"Fennel, carraway, and the color red; fennel, carraway, and the color red."*

Mackenzie came to the door when I rang, holding a big book of fairy tales. "We're reading. What's up?"

"I went to the library to look up the stuff the woman bought."

"And?"

"We need to talk."

Barnaby was right behind her, dressed in navy corduroy overalls and a navy and white striped T-shirt. Not a spot of red on him, I saw. "I wanna hear the end!" he said, pulling at Mackenzie's arm. "Come on, 'Kenzie. Read me the end!"

Mackenzie rolled her eyes. "I've got some things to tell you, too. But I'd better finish the story first."

We went into the living room and I sat and stared into the empty fireplace, thinking *fennel, carraway, and the color red,* while Mackenzie settled herself on the couch with Barnaby in her lap. "So every day Hansel held out the chicken bone for the witch to feel," she read.

" 'Hansel and Gretel'?" I asked.

She shrugged. "His other choice was 'Snow White.' "

So much for avoiding the subject of witches! I listened as she read and was amazed that I'd never thought that story was really scary when I was little. The whole point was that witches first lured little kids with candy and then baked them and ate them!

"Did the witch get all burned up in the oven?" Barnaby asked when Mackenzie had finished.

"All burned up," she assured him.

"Good!" he said. "No more witch."

"No more witch," Mackenzie agreed. "And no more witches. They're just from old, old stories."

"What about fairy godmothers?" he asked.

"They're just from stories, too."

"And wicked stepmothers?"

"Well—"

"Mackenzie," I said, "we need to talk."

"How about a little TV?" she asked Barnaby.

"It's Saturday," Barnaby reminded her. Mrs. Dawkins didn't believe in Saturday-morning cartoon shows. She said they were too violent and too commercial.

"Okay," Mackenzie said. "You can draw instead."

We got Barnaby settled at his little table and chair with a big pad of paper and some crayons. "Poo-doo wants to draw, too," he said. Mackenzie got another pad of paper, which he made her put on the floor along with a handful of crayons.

"We'll be right in the kitchen," she told him. "We'll make some cocoa."

"With baby 'mellows?" he asked.

"With baby marshmallows." We went into the kitchen. "Okay," she said, "you first."

So I told her what I'd found—all of it.

"Henbane," she said. "Parsley."

"She bought half a pound of parsley!"

"It's as bad as I thought. We've got to protect Barnaby. We can make him an amulet. We'll make a pouch out of cloth—like Mom makes to put the cinnamon and cloves and stuff in for mulled cider. He can wear it around his neck. We should have them, too."

I wasn't going to wear a pouch like that around my neck, but I guessed I could keep one in a pocket, or carry it in my backpack. Like insurance. The power of the mind, I reminded myself.

"We'll change his shirt, too. He can wear his red turtleneck."

"You said you had things to tell me, too. What?"

"I'll show you." She got her baby-sitting bag out and rooted through it. She pulled out a handkerchief for the amulets, a pack of shoelaces to tie Barnaby's up with, and one of her New Age audiotape catalogs. It was folded open and a section in the middle of the page was highlighted in yellow. "Read this," she said. "I mailed my order for it this morning."

I read what Mackenzie had highlighted. It told about a tape called "Psychic Self-Defense." "*Specific methods,*" it said, "*to dissolve curses, repel evil, and prevent psychic attack.*"

"Psychic attack? Do you mean somebody might have enough mind power to get into your mind and do something to it? Like a computer virus or something?"

Mackenzie shrugged. "I don't know. I never even noticed that tape before, but last night I was reading through the catalog to see if I could find something useful, and there it was. It practically jumped off the page at me. Look. It explains that you can visualize protective forces around yourself—or even somebody else. Forces like love and peace and harmony. I started doing that as soon as I read about it. I spent half an hour before I went to bed visualizing this wall, sort of, around Barnaby. It's a wall of love—like all made of valentines. And another one around our house, around Unicorn Catering and Mom and me. But I want the tape, too, because it tells how to dissolve curses."

I shook my head. It was as if I'd suddenly stumbled into a whole world I'd never known was there. And all this time, it had been all around me. Obviously lots of other people had known about it. There were books about it—and tapes.

"You'd better visualize a wall, too," Mackenzie said.

"Me? Why me?"

"I've been thinking," she said, "about you and algebra. You've always been good at school stuff—even math. All of a sudden, you can't understand it. Doesn't that seem awfully weird?"

"But I couldn't do algebra right from the beginning, way before we ever saw the old woman."

"Do the wall, anyway," Mackenzie said. "Maybe she's been watching us a lot longer than we know."

That I couldn't believe. The hat alone we'd have noticed. But cursed? I shivered. A wall would be a good idea. I decided to visualize a thick one. The woman had ordered an awful lot of parsley.

Parsley. I thought of all the times I'd eaten parsley buttered potatoes. And the times my dad told me I was supposed to eat the parsley they put on your plate at a restaurant. "Makes your breath sweet," he'd say. Some breath freshener. *The devil's oatmeal.* "Let's make the amulets," I said.

Mrs. Dawkins turned out to have both fennel and carraway seeds in her spice cabinet. We cut the handkerchief up and made three little packets with ten seeds of each kind. We closed them up with rubber bands and tied Barnaby's into the middle of a shoelace.

"Lookie, 'Kenzie," Barnaby said when we went into the living room to take it to him. "I drawed a big battle tank!"

Only Barnaby would recognize his drawing. To me, it looked like a deformed circle with squiggles at the bottom. If there was a gun on it, I couldn't tell where.

Mackenzie asked what Poo-doo had drawn and Barnaby looked at her as if she were crazy. "Dogs can't draw!" he said.

It was easy to get Barnaby to wear the amulet. Mackenzie told him he'd been promoted in the Unicorn Catering Auxiliary Task Force. Now he was a general. The amulet proved it. "And generals," she added, when she'd tied the shoelace around his neck, "always wear red."

So it was easy to get him to change into his red turtleneck, too. What wasn't so easy was the rest of the morning. Barnaby hadn't been to the park for more than a week. And when he had on his red shirt and his amulet and had put on his Auxiliary Task Force arm band and hat, he insisted on going there. Mackenzie offered to let him help make homemade Play-Doh. She even offered to let him break the rules and watch cartoons. His mouth got tighter and his frown got deeper. "I want to go to the park!" he insisted. "Generals get to say what they want. I want to go to the park."

She looked at me and I shrugged. "He's wearing the amulet," I said. "And the red shirt."

Mackenzie sighed. "A good baby-sitter doesn't let a child get his way like this," she whispered as Barnaby began stamping around the room shouting, "Park, park, park!"

"You should have thought of that before you promoted him to general," I said.

We went to the park.

10

———————●———————

Barnaby wanted Poo-doo to be a general, too, so Mackenzie had to explain that there could only be one
general or nobody would know who was boss. He settled for having Poo-doo made a captain. Then he insisted that we had to salute him and Poo-doo both.

He marched all the way to the park, stomping his
feet—as usual—and saying, "Hot-and-two-four, hot-
and-two-four" at the top of his voice. Mackenzie yelled
"Company halt!" at every street to get him to stop, and
then Barnaby made us salute him—and Poo-doo—
before we could cross. For a child who wasn't allowed
to have war toys, Barnaby had a very clear vision of the
military.

Through the din Barnaby was making, I brooded about the idea of a psychic attack. Could somebody really get into your mind? Break into your brain and steal thoughts or ideas? Or put other ones in? I wondered if you'd know if you were under psychic attack. Would you hear a strange voice whispering in your head, telling you to do what you didn't want to do? If your own mind wasn't safe, what was?

There were lots of people in the park. It made me feel better. Spells and curses and psychic attacks didn't seem like much of a threat in public in the bright sunlight with all those kids and parents and dogs around.

Barnaby headed straight for the sandbox. "Captain Poo-doo wants to stay with you," he said on the way. "He doesn't like sand in his eyes."

"Sand isn't for throwing," Mackenzie reminded him.

"I know," he said, and stepped in among the other little kids who were busily digging and molding. Mackenzie hadn't brought her baby-sitting bag, so we didn't have his shovel and bucket. There was at least one person on every bench, so we sat down on the grass under a big orange maple tree.

We didn't get to sit there long. A little girl was molding castles with a cottage cheese carton. Barnaby watched her for a few minutes. Then he must have decided cottage cheese cartons were a good idea and that she ought to share. "Gimme!" he said.

She held the carton over her head to keep it away.

"I'm a general," Barnaby said. "You have to do what I say."

She hit him over the head with the carton. Barnaby threw a handful of sand. Another kid dumped a whole bucketful of sand over Barnaby's head. By the time we and the two mothers had gotten the three of them separated, Barnaby was yelling at the top of his lungs that everybody had to do what generals told them to do.

"Maybe it isn't too late to demote him," I muttered to Mackenzie as we shooed him, protesting, toward the swings.

Instead of answering, she jerked her head to the right. I looked. The old woman was sitting on the end of a bench where no one had been a few moments before. She had on the purple hat again, an orange and green paisley dress, and that same patchwork jacket. Her long white hair was done in a single braid that hung over her shoulder, and a big black canvas bag was at her feet. She was watching the kids in the sandbox. I looked away. For some reason, I didn't want to take a chance on meeting her eyes. *Henbane,* I thought. *Parsley.*

Mackenzie put Barnaby into one of the baby swings. "Push me!" he said. "High, high, high!"

"Please," Mackenzie reminded him.

"Generals don't say please," he said.

I glanced at the old woman again. She was looking our way now.

"I don't like this," I said as Mackenzie pushed and

Barnaby swept forward. I waited till he came back and Mackenzie pushed him forward again. "She's watching us." Swing back, push forward. "We should get"—swing back, push forward—"away from here."

Mackenzie nodded. "I've got a feeling." Swing back, push forward. "We should follow her—and find out where she lives."

"Oh no," I said.

"Yes," she said.

"Not me," I said.

"Then we'll go—by ourselves," she said.

If there was ever a time I needed to take a stand against Mackenzie, this was it. Whether the woman was a witch or not, we couldn't go around spying on her. It was probably illegal. And maybe dangerous. What if she saw us?

"Over my dead body," I said.

"Poo-doo wants to go down the slide," Barnaby said.

Mackenzie stopped the swing, slid up the bar, and lifted him out. He and Poo-doo marched toward the slide and we followed. I glanced back. The old woman had shifted her position on the bench a little to keep watching him.

"Tell you what," Mackenzie said quietly. "We'll leave the playground in a couple of minutes and hide in the bushes down the hill. If she stays where she is, watching the other kids, we'll just take Barnaby home. But if she gets up to follow us, we follow her instead."

I thought about it. She probably wouldn't follow us. After all, there was a whole playground full of kids to watch. But if she did, it would pretty much mean she wasn't watching just any kid, she was watching Barnaby—and us, too, maybe. "Well—"

"It's only fair, Case," Mackenzie said. "If she can follow us, we can follow her."

"Okay."

"General Barnaby, sir!" she said as Barnaby came barreling down the slide. She saluted. I saluted. Barnaby stood up and saluted back. "The commander in chief has sent you an order. You must do what he says."

Barnaby frowned. "Do not. I'm the general!"

"Generals have to take orders from the commander in chief. *Everybody* has to take orders from him. He's the biggest boss."

Barnaby looked suspicious. "What orders?"

"There's somebody in the park who might be a *spy*," Mackenzie said, her voice low and conspiratorial. "And the Unicorn Auxiliary Task Force, under General Barnaby Dawkins, has been ordered to follow her and find out if she is one or not. The commander in chief says it's very, very important. But only the general can order the task force to undertake this mission."

I didn't think Barnaby understood half the words Mackenzie was using.

"What's a spy?" he asked.

"A—well—a bad person," Mackenzie said.

"Who might be bad?"

"That woman over there," Mackenzie said. "In the purple hat. We have to follow wherever she goes and be very, very careful that she doesn't see us."

"She isn't going," Barnaby pointed out.

"She will. First we'll go and then she'll go. We'll hide and then we'll follow her."

"Like hide-and-seek," Barnaby said.

"Like that," Mackenzie said. "It's a secret hide-and-seek mission."

"Okay," the general said.

"Time to go," Mackenzie said loudly. When Barnaby had gotten Captain Poo-doo in place beside him, she shouted, "Company, move out!" and Barnaby started his marching chant again—"Hot-and-two-four." We marched down the path the way we had come, making so much noise, the whole world had to know we were leaving.

When we'd gone around some bushes and were out of sight of the playground, Mackenzie pulled us off the path. "Now we wait till she gets up to leave, then we follow her."

We waited a minute or two, and then Mackenzie told Barnaby to be very quiet and crept into the bushes to a place where she could see the old woman without being seen herself.

I was almost sure the woman wasn't going to follow

us. In fact, I closed my eyes and willed her to stay where she was.

"Hsst." It was Mackenzie. I could see her arm beckoning through the browning leaves of the bush she was hiding in. "She's getting up. And coming this way. Get over here with me, and stay quiet!"

"Did you hear that, Barnaby?" I whispered. "Mackenzie says to stay quiet."

"Generals are always quiet," Barnaby said. He stomped his way in among the branches.

I stopped him. "Your feet have to be quiet, too."

He leaned down and told Poo-doo to keep his feet quiet, and we made our way in under the bushes until we were crouched next to Mackenzie.

When the woman went by on the path, heading for Monument Avenue, we waited a little while and then followed. "What if she looks behind her?" I whispered to Mackenzie. "If we stay close enough to see where she's going, she'll be able to see us if she looks around."

"If she looks, we just pretend to be walking along. We pretend we don't even know she's there."

But she didn't look back a single time. She just walked out of the park, down Monument Avenue, and up Ridge. We had to stop a lot because she was walking so slowly. It was all we could do not to catch up with her.

Finally, she turned in toward a yellow brick apartment building set between two big houses. "Is that her house?" Barnaby asked.

"It's an apartment building," Mackenzie said.

"Now what do we do?" I asked.

"You walk on past. I'm going to follow her in, try to see which apartment is hers."

I stopped. "Oh no you don't. You can't go in."

"I want to go, too," Barnaby said. "Generals get to go in."

We stopped on the sidewalk in front of the house next door. "It's all of us or nobody," I said. And I meant it. I was pretty sure she'd give up the idea, since all three of us going in would be much too conspicuous.

"Okay, all of us." She told Barnaby he had to be very, very, very quiet, then started across the lawn toward the apartment building's front door.

I couldn't let her go alone, and I knew Barnaby would fuss if he couldn't go with her. So I followed, clutching Barnaby's hand. Inside, there was a dark lobby that wasn't much more than a hall. Dingy doors with numbers on them opened off it. There wasn't anybody to be seen. But we were in time to hear a door close in the shadows at the far end. Mackenzie put out her hand to tell us to stay put and hurried toward the sound.

That's when I noticed the delicious spicy smell of something baking. It was coming from the end of the hall—just where Mackenzie was headed. "Ginger-

bread," Barnaby said. "That smells like gingerbread."
I shushed him.

Suddenly, from behind the door that Mackenzie had crept up to, came a scream. It was high and shrill and piercing. Mackenzie jumped back as another scream followed the first.

The next thing I knew, Barnaby and I were on the sidewalk outside the apartment building. I didn't even remember getting there. Mackenzie arrived about half a second later. "Did you hear that?" she asked.

"You think I'm deaf?"

"I smelled gingerbread," Barnaby said, his eyes enormous. "Just like in Hansel and Gretel. She isn't a bad-person spy, 'Kenzie. She's a bad-person witch!"

Mackenzie looked at her watch. "Time to get going," she said. "Your mother's probably home already, Barnaby, wondering where you are."

"We can tell her we found a real, true gingerbread witch," Barnaby said.

"No, no, General," Mackenzie said. "We won't tell anybody. This was a secret mission, remember?"

11

———●———

We took Barnaby home, reminding him all the way not to say anything about a witch or a spy or a bad person, to his mother or anybody else. Then we headed for Mackenzie's house.

"Police! We have to go to the police," Mackenzie said as we went.

"We can't. What would we tell them—that she's a witch? First, we don't know for sure she is. Second, they wouldn't believe us even if we did. Third, she hasn't *done* anything."

"Somebody screamed in her apartment."

"It could have been on television."

"It sounded real," Mackenzie said. She was right, but

I didn't want to think about it. "And what about the curse? What about Unicorn Catering and following us?"

"You can't prove a curse, Mackenzie. For that matter, you can't prove she was following us. If we went to the police, the only thing we could prove is that *we* were following *her*. We can't tell the police!"

Mackenzie kicked at the pavement with her rope-soled shoes. "We have to tell *somebody!*"

We decided to tell her mother.

But when we got to the house, we didn't get a chance. Mrs. Brewster came out of the kitchen, wiping her hands on her apron, pushing the damp hair off her face. The sound of the television drifted in from the kitchen with the smell of baking. "Where have you been? I've called the Dawkins house three times! My life is falling apart. *Falling apart!*"

Mrs. Brewster looked sort of gray. There were deep lines between her eyebrows and around her mouth.

Mackenzie started to explain. "We went to the park, Mom. And we have something to tell—"

"Casey, I hate like anything to ask again, but I wonder if you could stay this afternoon and help out."

I nodded.

"Thanks. The Tofu Lasagna was a bust last night—none of *those* people will ever hire me, either." She turned to Mackenzie. "I got a notice from the bank in the mail this morning; the telephone check bounced. And the child-support check is late again. And I've got a bill due next week at my produce supplier. If I don't get things turned around, Unicorn Catering will be out of business by the end of the month! We'll be on the street by Christmas. On the street!"

"Mom—" Mackenzie started.

Her mother ran the back of her hand across her forehead and went on. "I interviewed another applicant this morning. Someone my age. She could read recipes. She could cook. But she wouldn't work evenings and weekends. Can you believe it? She applied for a catering job and wouldn't work evenings and weekends!"

Mrs. Brewster took a breath and went on before Mackenzie could even open her mouth.

"I've got a dessert buffet tonight. Thank heavens *somebody* still gives dessert buffets." She pointed toward the kitchen. "There are puffs in the oven, the batter is ready for a double chocolate amaretto torte, and I'm about to start on the apricot buttercream squares. I've lined up a server for tonight. *But now I need help!*"

So we helped. With the television droning quietly through a forties colorized movie and a sports program full of car racing and boxing, we helped. It wasn't until the torte was finished, the buttercream squares were cooling in the refrigerator, and Mackenzie and I were putting the custard into the puffs while Mrs. Brewster drizzled them with chocolate to make éclairs that Mackenzie dared to bring up the old woman.

92

"I'm sorry we were late getting home today," she began. "But I had a *feeling* while we were in the park, so we had to follow—"

"Oh, sweetie, not those feelings again," her mother said.

"Mom, you have to listen. It's important."

"I know they seem important to you, hon, but you mustn't overdramatize. You can't put your feelings ahead of good common sense."

Mackenzie put down the puff she had just filled. I kept working. "You didn't think it was overdramatizing when it turned out Prudie really was stealing from the company, just like I told you. Just like my *feeling* said."

Mrs. Brewster paused, holding her chocolate spoon above a half-finished puff. "All right. That time, your feeling was right. I don't know how it was right, but it was right. That doesn't mean every little twinge you get is some absolute truth from another dimension." She went back to drizzling. "It doesn't make sense."

"Mom, listen. This is every bit as important as the time with Prudie. Maybe more important. Our whole lives could depend on it."

Mrs. Brewster put her spoon into the chocolate bowl with a sigh. "All right. I'll listen. What's going on?"

"There's a witch in Maple Park, and—"

That's as far as she got. Mrs. Brewster's reaction was just what I knew would happen if we tried to go to the police. You can't go around saying there's a witch in town. Most people don't know about henbane and parsley. They don't know about covens and black magic and scientific evidence that curses can work. They hear the word *witch* and right away think about black pointy hats and broomsticks.

"Mackenzie Brewster, I've had just about all I can stand," her mother said. "Dr. Antoine said I should let you alone with this New Age stuff. She said the meditation was good for you and visualization couldn't hurt, and maybe you really are a little psychic. She said we couldn't know how much of what you were tuning into was real and how much might come from the trauma of the divorce." Mrs. Brewster started pacing. "So I let you decorate your room. I let you wear those clothes. And I don't mind. Really I don't.

"But, Mackenzie, your father has been gone almost two years now. It's time you were getting over it. We have enough to worry about keeping a roof over our heads."

"That's just it," Mackenzie broke in. "I think the witch has put a curse on Unicorn Catering. That's why everything's going wrong. If we can't break the curse, we really could be on the street by Christmas. And she's been following us. Watching Barnaby. And—"

"Witches! Curses! Casey," Mrs. Brewster said, turning to me. *"Witches?"*

I told her about the research I'd done. At least she listened. She sat down on the tall kitchen stool and listened. Mackenzie threw in whatever I forgot, until we'd told her everything, even about the amulets and the red turtleneck. "I know it sounds crazy," I finished. "But there's all that stuff about the power of the mind, and a whole lot of it even scientists can't explain. What if it isn't crazy?"

"There's something evil about her, Mom. I know it." I was glad Mackenzie didn't mention that we'd followed the woman. I didn't think her mother would take that very well.

Mrs. Brewster sat very still for a minute and didn't say anything. A beer commercial came on television. She looked around the kitchen and sighed. Then she looked back and forth between me and Mackenzie. "I don't know what to say. There are people who say they're witches. I accept that. And maybe they really do believe they can cast spells and put curses on people. But I can't believe those spells or curses work. And I can't believe an old woman in Maple Park, Ohio, has put a curse on my business. It feels like a curse to me, too, sometimes, but why would anybody do such a thing?"

Mackenzie sighed and picked up a pastry puff to fill it. "What if you're wrong?" she said, her voice very low.

"And what if *you* are? These feelings could be left-overs from the divorce, blown up by that active imagination of yours. You can't go accusing some old woman of being a witch or putting curses on people. You might do real damage. There are lots of superstitious people, even now. Hundreds of years ago, innocent women got burned at the stake because of accusations just like that. I don't want to hear another word about it."

"But Mom—"

Mrs. Brewster stood up. "No buts, Mackenzie. You can't live your life according to feelings you don't even understand. Unicorn Catering is in trouble, all right, but we aren't going to save it by researching witchcraft. We need to focus every scrap of time and energy we have on good old-fashioned hard work. It's going to take both of us to get through this, and anyone else I can get to help."

She sighed. "There has to be a literate, sane, sensible person out there somewhere. I will find that person eventually. In the meantime, I can't have you off on a witch-hunt."

"But Mom—"

"I said no buts. If you're really so worried, keep those amulets with you. Bring Barnaby over here after school. That'll keep both of you safe and it'll keep you here, where you can help me. Until we get past this crisis, I need you to concentrate every ounce of energy and whatever psychic power you have on *us*. On Unicorn Catering. On survival!"

Mrs. Brewster's eyes glittered, and I could see that she was very close to tears.

Mackenzie swallowed hard. So did I. It's amazing how catching tears can be. "All right," she said finally. "I'll help whenever you need me. And I'll visualize good things for us. Casey will, too, won't you, Case?"

I nodded.

Mrs. Brewster brushed her hair out of her face and smiled. "Okay. Thanks." An announcer on the television told us to stay tuned for the local evening news. Mrs. Brewster looked at her watch. "Good Lord, look at the time. The temporary-services woman'll be here in half an hour." She glanced toward the TV screen. "Oh, terrific!" she screeched. "Now she's been promoted to weekend anchor!"

A woman's face filled the television screen, blond hair swooped over her forehead in a studied, windblown look. "The newest member of the weekend news team—Eileen Phillips," the announcer said. It was the woman from the "News at Noon," the one Mr. Brewster had run off with—Mackenzie's stepmother. The camera panned back to get the whole news desk, the man with the mustache who does sports, the gray-haired weatherman, and in the center, Eileen Phillips, her white teeth gleaming above a vibrant purple blouse.

Mackenzie leapt across the room and turned off the TV. The Channel 8 weekend news team dwindled to a white dot and evaporated.

Mrs. Brewster tore off her apron and flung it on the counter. "Finish the éclairs," she said, her voice sounding half-strangled. "I've got to get dressed."

12

———————•———————

That night when I went home, I thought a lot about
what Mrs. Brewster had said. And I wanted to believe
it. If Mackenzie's feelings were really about the divorce
and money worries instead of psychic messages, we
didn't have to think about magic and curses. But I
couldn't get what I'd read out of my mind, or the
scream that had come from that old woman's apartment.

My dreams that night were weird and terrible. They
were all full of witches and screaming and food. In one,
I was stuck in a giant éclair and somebody was eating
it from the other end, huge teeth getting closer and
closer. When I woke up from that one, I couldn't get
back to sleep until I put the math tape on my Walkman

and drifted away on the sound of ocean waves. It was probably because of the subliminal math messages that in the next dream Mrs. Mendez was putting pins in a voodoo doll with frizzy hair.

On Sunday afternoon when Mackenzie called to ask me to come over so we could put our mental powers together in a joint visualization, I was happy to go. At least it was something positive to do.

When I got there, the only light in Mackenzie's room came from the fiber-optic lamp on her dresser. The hollow sounds of Mayan flutes floated out of the speakers of her tape recorder. In the shadows, I could just make her out, sitting on the floor with her legs folded in the lotus position.

"Did you start without me?"

"I've been meditating," she said. "To get ready." She paused the tape recorder and the clay flutes quit.

"How'd the dessert buffet go last night?"

"Great. Maybe my anticurse visualizations are starting to work."

I didn't remind her that desserts had never been a problem for Unicorn Catering. "So—what are we supposed to be visualizing? Pots of money and lots of success for your mom?"

"Let's start with protection."

"Okay." Maybe it would work against nightmares, too. "So, what do we do?"

"The same sort of thing I told you about before.

100

Make pictures in your mind and concentrate on them hard enough to make them true. We'll do it together, combine forces. Sit on the floor facing me, and close enough so our knees and hands can touch. That'll make a circle of visualization. It'll be stronger." She unpaused the music and the flutes filled the room again.

I sat down and crossed my legs, Indian-style. Our knees touched. I imitated what she was doing with her hands, resting them palms up on my knees and touching my thumbs with my middle fingers, being sure our hands were touching, too. "Okay. Now what?"

"Now visualize some kind of protection. Start with Barnaby."

"What kind of protection?"

"Any kind you want. A fence. A wall. A shield. Anything. Get it into your mind, and then *concentrate*."

I closed my eyes and envisioned Barnaby in a full miniature suit of armor, with a red plume on the helmet. Then I imagined tiny doggie armor for Poo-doo. It made me want to laugh. This wasn't supposed to be funny.

"Now do the same for the rest of us. Me and you and Mom, too."

I couldn't. The idea of all of us in armor was too ridiculous. Anyway, armor was to protect people from arrows, not from magic. Then I thought of a picture in an old storybook of mine. "Do you remember 'Sleeping Beauty'? Where the wall of thorns grew up all around her castle so that nobody could get near her for a hundred years? That was magic. How about that?"

"Great! You visualize that. I'm doing a sort of a force field—a red glow all around us." She closed her eyes, then opened them again. "And while you're doing it, think peace and love and harmony."

I breathed deeply a few times and closed my eyes. The flute music filled my mind. I put Barnaby and Poo-doo, armor and all, and Mackenzie and her mother and me into the picture I remembered from the book. We were surrounded by rosebushes. The roses were white. And red. Like peace and love. I concentrated on the thorny branches, seeing them grow longer and fatter, intertwining with each other. They grew higher, gradually shutting out everything else—a perfect wall of protection. I listened to the flutes and kept that wall in my mind. Protection. White roses. Red roses. Peace, love, harmony. Peace, love—

The prince from my storybook came riding toward the dense wall of thorns on a huge white horse, a sword raised above his head. He hacked at the bushes, and rose petals flew into the air, catching the breeze, drifting away. The prince hacked on, broken branches falling to the ground. An opening appeared in the tangled branches, and I saw his face. Howie Mankowitz.

I jolted awake.

Mackenzie was looking at me. "You okay?"

"Sure," I said. I didn't want her to know I'd fallen asleep. It had to have been a dream. Howie Mankowitz?

"Casey, while I was visualizing that force field, I got one of my feelings."

"What about?"

"The witch. It wasn't just general evil this time. Barnaby was part of it. And Mom. There *is* a connection between her and us. I'm *not* just imagining it. This was as strong a feeling as any I've ever had."

I understood about meditating, even though I couldn't do it. I understood about visualizing, even though I had a little trouble controlling my images. But I'd never understood Mackenzie's feelings. "Explain how your feelings happen," I said. "I want to know what it's like."

Mackenzie unfolded her legs, so I had to move, too. My knees had gotten stiff. I was glad to get up and move to the chair. Mackenzie flipped on the overhead light and turned off the tape recorder. She sat on the bed, frowning.

"It doesn't always happen the same way. Sometimes it's just what I said—a feeling. You know, like when you're getting mad or scared, you just *feel* mad or scared. That time, I knew I was going to be able to go to Columbus, it was like that. I just felt—for sure—that I was. It felt as sure as if it had already happened. The way you know something that happened yesterday. Only it wasn't clear like that. I didn't know *what* was going to happen to let me go. Just something.

"Other times I get pictures—images. I *saw* Prudie

taking something out of Mom's cash box and putting it in her purse."

"You saw it? Like in a movie?"

Mackenzie shook her head. "More like a dream. And I didn't actually see the money. I just saw her take something. I saw the cash box, though, and her purse. So I figured she had to be stealing. Turned out I was right."

I felt goose bumps going up my arms again. How would I feel if things I felt or dreams I dreamed started coming true?

"Sometimes there are words—I see them or hear them. That's what happened with the old woman the first time. I could see her, especially that hat she wears, but I *heard* the word *witch*."

"So what was *this* feeling like?"

Mackenzie shuddered. "It was like a dream again. Sort of mixed up. I saw the woman, and *she was with Barnaby*. It felt like she was trying to take him away from me." Mackenzie rubbed her hands together as if they were cold. "It was awful, Case. Then I saw her with Mom. Right with her. And over everything, this feeling of evil."

"You think it's the curse?"

"I don't know." Mackenzie ran her hand through her hair. "She and Mom were together. And Mom's never even seen her. So maybe it's something that is *going* to happen. Something in the future."

"What can we do?"

She shrugged. "I don't know that, either. All I know for sure is that she really is connected to us somehow. To Barnaby and Mom, and maybe you and me, too."

My goose bumps got worse. I didn't envy Mackenzie's psychic powers anymore, not even a little. What if you could know bad things before they happened but couldn't do anything to change them? What if you just had to wait for them to happen? It would be hundreds of times worse than not knowing.

"I guess I'll just go on visualizing the force field. You, too, Casey. Keep visualizing protection—for all of us."

I nodded. At least I could try.

"And wear red."

13

On Wednesday, I began to believe in visualization. I didn't know if it could work against witches or not, but what I'd seen at Mackenzie's house came true right there at Maple Park Middle School—in the library in fifth-period study hall.

I was sitting there, staring at the math quiz Mrs. Mendez had handed back. The big red *D* seemed to be burning a hole in my brain. I might not be as smart as school people think, but I'd never gotten a *D* before in my life! The idea of a witch's curse was beginning to sound better to me than the other explanation—the complete disintegration of my brain—when I heard my name. There, standing next to me, was Howie Mankowitz.

"I noticed you're having a hard time with algebra," he said.

I couldn't deny it. There was that *D* for the whole world to see.

"Maybe I can help. I know you can do it, you're so good at everything else."

And just like the knight hacking his way through the wall of thorns, Howie Mankowitz came to my rescue. He sat down with me and we got out our math books and notebooks, and in forty minutes most of the tangles in my brain were gone. Just gone. It wasn't like algebra with Mrs. Mendez or Ian. When Howie explained things, I understood them. The numbers and letters fell into place. It was like a miracle.

Then, when study hall was almost over, he said something amazing. "It's the power of the mind."

"What?" I asked. "What did you say?"

"I said, it's the power of the mind! You could do it all the time, but you didn't know it. You've had a mental block." I noticed that he got two little lines over his nose when he was being serious. They were sort of cute. "For some reason, you've been thinking you couldn't do algebra. So you couldn't."

"My brother, Ian, says I'm a dunce about algebra."

"See? If somebody says you can't do it, especially if you already *think* you can't, then you can't. People can explain and explain, but you can't hear them. You make sort of a mental wall and the ideas can't get through."

107

A mental wall of thorns, I thought.

"It works the other way, too. I knew you could do it, so that helped you think you could. And what you think you *can* do, you can. It's the power of the mind!"

I told him about the math tapes. He'd never heard of subliminal tapes, but he listened to everything I'd read about how they're supposed to work. Then he shook his head. "All those messages probably couldn't do any good because they couldn't get into your brain. They kept bouncing off what you *really* thought—that you were a dunce in math. You need to work on your self-esteem, Casey. You're really . . ." He paused, as if he was looking for the right word. ". . . better than you think." I didn't know if *better* was the word he'd wanted, but it would do.

The bell rang then and we had to gather up our stuff. I noticed his hands—not very big, but graceful in a strong sort of way. I supposed they could hold a sword.

I wanted to tell Mackenzie about how my visualization had come true, and what Howie had said about the power of the mind, but I didn't get a chance. Things weren't getting any better for Unicorn Catering in spite of the force field she was visualizing, and she was getting as frazzled as her mom. More, I guess, because her mom didn't have to worry about the witch, and Mackenzie kept thinking that the witch was somehow getting closer all the time.

Three more job interviews had gone bust, so there

still wasn't a full-time assistant. And even though she'd been trying new recipes out steadily, the fliers Mrs. Brewster had ordered, advertising gourmet health-food dinners, came back from the printer before she'd found even one main dish she thought was good enough to offer.

Meanwhile, Barnaby was getting fed up with having to stay either at his house or Mackenzie's. He wanted to go to the library, to the fire station, to the park and the fountain and the pet store.

The man with the low cholesterol had hired Unicorn Catering for a dinner party Saturday night because he loved the macadamia wings. But since a lot of his friends had been at the Freidels' party, he wanted a health-food main dish, too.

That morning, a gorgeous sunny fall morning, Mackenzie and her mother were trying out their last hope, Linguine Brewster. This was a euphemism for Baked Linguine with Turkey and Eggplant Sauce, which for some reason Mrs. Brewster thought sounded perfect. It had four stars in the cookbook, so I guess that's what she was going by.

Mackenzie begged me to come help, so I put on my red sweatshirt, stuck my pouch of fennel and carraway seeds into my back pocket, and went. I was getting to be very fast at chopping and slicing, as long as the pieces didn't have to be too small or too even.

"Park, park, park!" Barnaby started yelling about an

hour after I got there. He was stomping around and around the kitchen. "Me and Poo-doo wanna go to the park!"

I was slicing eggplant, and Mackenzie, her hair tied back with a red scarf, had been trying to get Barnaby to help her build a block city over in the corner out of the way. Luckily, their kitchen is one of the great big eat-in kinds, so there was room for all of us—but only if Barnaby stayed out from underfoot. Now, he was definitely *not* out from underfoot.

"Barn, come and see the city I built," Mackenzie said in her sweetest "lure the little boy" voice. "It needs a tall, *tall* skyscraper. I need you to build it for me."

Barnaby's fat, dimpled cheeks were pinched and his mouth made that flat, tight line. "The general says park. It's a 'mergency mission!" He stamped his feet together and stood straight and stiff. With his red shirt and his unicorn hat and his fists doubled up at his sides, he looked like something out of a training film for miniature marines. "If we don't go, Poo-doo might bite somebody," he added, his voice ominous. "I could say no, but he might, anyway."

"Captain Poo-doo's too good to do that," Mackenzie said. "You did a great job training him, General, sir!" She snapped him a salute. This did nothing to mollify him.

"Park!" he repeated, and stamped one foot and then the other.

Mrs. Brewster stood at the stove, stirring the sauce for the wings. She sighed and brushed the hair back from her face. "Mackenzie . . ." she said, and let it hang in the air for a minute. I glanced over at her. Her face was pale again, and there were dark circles under her eyes. "I have exactly"—she glanced up at the clock over the sink—"nine hours and forty-three minutes before I have to have Mr. Sternhagen's dinner ready. In that time, I have to taste-test the linguine and, if it isn't too awful, make four pans of it. We won't even consider what I'll do if the stuff turns out to be inedible." She waved her spoon in the air and dripped sauce on the stove and counter. "Besides that, I have to chop three heads of cauliflower and four bunches of broccoli, turn two pounds of carrots into sticks, cut up the star fruits and kiwis and three pineapples, wash four quarts of strawberries—"

Mackenzie interrupted before she could finish. "I know, Mom." She pushed herself to her feet and came to attention, stamping her feet as Barnaby had. "General Barnaby, sir!" she said, saluting him.

"What?" said Barnaby suspiciously.

"There's another emergency mission in the back-yard. My old sandbox is out by the swing set. The Auxiliary Task Force needs a bunker built in the sand. And roads. Very important roads."

Barnaby frowned. "Do you got a shovel? And a dump truck?"

Mackenzie nodded. "Yes, sir. Right in my bag. You won't have to share it with anybody. And nobody will throw sand in your eyes."

Barnaby leaned down and held a whispered conversation with Poo-doo. "Captain Poo-doo says okay," he said.

Mackenzie and I and her mother all heaved sighs of relief. Mackenzie and Barnaby went outside and I went back to slicing eggplant.

Mrs. Brewster and I worked in silence, the TV droning a program about how to paint landscapes. She boiled the noodles and sauteed onions for the sauce.

When the linguine was in the oven, baking, and I was washing cauliflower, Mrs. Brewster let out a shriek. "I don't believe it!" she yelled, smacking her forehead with the palm of one hand. "I totally forgot to buy the macadamia nuts!" She looked wildly around the kitchen. "That does it! I'll never get everything done in time now. It'll take at least two people working non-stop—"

"You go ahead to the store. Mackenzie can come in and help," I assured her. "Now that the linguine's in, everything else that needs doing is stuff we've done before."

"What about Barnaby?"

"He can stay out there by himself," I said. "The yard's fenced in, and we'll be right here. We can leave the door open so he can call if he needs us. He'll be fine."

When Barnaby had assured her that he'd be okay and would be very careful and guard the yard, Mrs. Brewster went off to the store. "If anybody comes, Poo-doo'll eat 'em up," he had promised her.

We left Poo-doo patrolling the fence—I could almost see him by now—and Barnaby shoveling sand, singing at the top of his lungs and a little off-key, "This old man, he played one—"

Now that we were alone in the kitchen, I told Mackenzie I was worried about her mother. "What happens if the eggplant stuff is awful? What'll she do? I think she's right on the edge."

To my surprise, she just smiled. "Don't worry. While I was building that block city, I suddenly got this image of double rainbows, and Mom right in the middle of them." She picked up a bunch of broccoli and a knife. "It's the first *good* feeling I've had in ages. Tonight's dinner is going to be fine. I know it."

"You should tell your mom and save her all this worrying."

"You know she doesn't trust my feelings."

"What about the *other* one?" I asked. "The one about the—witch?" I still didn't like to use the word.

She shrugged. "I've been visualizing the force field. Maybe it's working."

113

While we finished cutting the vegetables and arranging them on the platters, I told her about Howie Mankowitz. She didn't pay much attention, though. She never did when the subject was guys. The divorce had seriously warped her attitude.

"Okay," she said when we'd finished the vegetables. "Fruit next." She picked up a box of strawberries and set it down again. "Barnaby!" she said. "I don't hear him anymore."

I listened. He'd been singing loud enough to be heard over the TV. Now there was only the man saying, "Use your almighty big brush."

"I'd better just go check," she said. "It's not like him to be quiet."

I had just dumped the first strawberries into the collander when Mackenzie came back. She looked worse than her mother. In her hand was Barnaby's amulet.

"This was in the sandbox. He's gone! The gate is hanging open!"

We rushed back out into the yard. There was nowhere he could be hiding. "I don't know how he got the gate open," Mackenzie said. "I never could when *I* was little."

We ran out the gate and around to the front of the house. He wasn't anywhere to be seen. "He doesn't have his protection!" Mackenzie wailed. "We've got to find him fast. You go that way," she said, pointing to the left, "and I'll go the other way."

We ran to the opposite ends of the block. I checked out driveways and yards as I went. No Barnaby. I hurried back to Mackenzie's house. She was back, too, shaking her head.

"What'll we do?" I asked.

Mackenzie didn't answer. She was standing very still, her eyes closed. She breathed deeply and slowly. I just waited. If we'd ever needed Mackenzie's psychic powers, we needed them now.

"I'm getting something," she said.

I stayed quiet. I didn't want to make static.

"Oh no!"

"What? What?" My heart was beating like crazy.

"She's got him! I see them together, Case. She's got him!"

"Where are they?" I asked. "Can you see that?"

Mackenzie didn't say anything for what seemed like hours. "Animals," she said finally. "I see animals and a big bird." She took another deep breath and there was another pause. "And in the background, there are shelves lined with bottles. Bottles of herbs."

"The pet shop!" I said. "And the health-food store next to it."

"That's it! She must have found him in the yard and lured him away by promising to take him to the pet shop. You know he can't resist the pet shop.''

"What'll we do?''

"The police! They're right there in the square. If she's got him in the pet shop, we can catch her. That's all the proof they'll need!''

"What if she's gone by the time you get there?''

Mackenzie frowned. "She might take him to her apartment. Listen, Casey, you go there. Don't get too close. Just someplace where you can see if she comes. If she does, and if she's got Barn, get right to a phone and call the police. That way, we'll have her covered both places.''

She didn't even wait for me to agree. She just took off, running in the direction of the square, her hair flying out behind her, her baggy pants flapping.

I stood for a minute, trying to decide what to do. What if the woman *had* left the pet shop already? What if I went to her apartment and she saw me? I did not want to go there by myself! I took a deep breath to try to calm myself, patted my back pocket, pulled down my red sweatshirt, and started walking. Even now, I couldn't help but do what Mackenzie wanted me to do.

As I went, I visualized that big thorny hedge again, full of roses. "Peace,'' I muttered under my breath. "Love. Harmony. Protection.''

14

I tried to keep the image of the thorn wall in my mind as I walked toward the apartment house where the old woman lived, but it kept slipping. In its place, other pictures would come. There was the woman, following us down to the duck pond. There was the page from the witch gardening book with the parsley plant. I kept blinking, as if that could turn the pictures off, or change them. I tried to picture the thorn wall growing up and over them. Instead, I got the image of the boiling cauldron and the body of the little boy. "Peace, love, protection," I muttered, and kept walking.

When I got close enough to see the apartment building, it looked the same way it had the day we'd first followed the old woman. Just an ordinary narrow yellow brick building set between two big old Victorian houses. Hardly sinister. Hardly a place you'd expect to find a witch, even a modern witch.

I stood behind a tree, sort of leaning against it, and watched. No sign of life. No woman in a purple hat and no Barnaby. I waited. And watched. And waited. Nobody went in or came out. I began to feel conspicuous. What if somebody was watching *me,* wondering what I was doing there? I looked up and down the street. The only people outside were a couple of kids riding tricycles about four houses down. If the woman was bringing Barnaby this way, she wasn't in sight.

Then it occurred to me that they might already be here. How would I know? I couldn't tell by watching the front door. The woman's apartment was at the back of the building. The only thing to do, I decided, was go back there and see if I could get a look inside.

So, with my neck hairs fizzing and goose bumps popping up all over me, I walked very casually down the driveway to the parking area at the back. Nothing there, either. A couple of cars, a couple of empty parking spaces, and a dumpster. I went around behind the dumpster and peered at the building. There was a side entrance off the driveway, but back here there were just high woven board fences surrounding little yards outside the two rear apartments. The one I wanted was the one on the far side.

118

I glanced around. There didn't seem to be anybody watching. I slipped along the first fence. There was a space between the two. Against the old woman's fence were two garbage cans and lots of big, dirty ceramic flowerpots stacked upside down. Next to them were half-full plastic bags of peat moss and topsoil and bark chips.

I crept closer to the fence. No sound. But somebody was cooking nearby. A wonderful chickeny smell filled the air. I went all the way along the fence around the old woman's backyard. Still nothing. There was a gate—latched. I didn't dare touch it. There was a window in the apartment wall on the other side, but it was too high to see into. So I went back and looked at the flowerpots. There were three stacks of them, one higher than the next.

If I was very careful, I might be able to use them like steps. I could climb up and peek over the top of the fence. The woman probably wasn't at home, I told myself. She was at the pet shop with Barnaby, even now being arrested by the police Mackenzie had brought. I was just going to peek in and make sure, that was all. Nothing to worry about. If they weren't there, nothing would happen except I'd get a glimpse of her apartment, maybe see if there was anything suspicious there. And if they were—I'd just jump back down and go call the police. Simple. And perfectly safe.

I grabbed hold of the fence and stepped carefully

119

onto the first pile of pots. Then up onto the next. Now I could get my hands to the top of the fence. I stepped onto the third pile and started to peek over the top.

Then a whole bunch of things seemed to happen all at once. There was a rustle on the other side of the fence. Then a thump, and I was staring directly into a gigantic black furry face with green eyes. A black cat had jumped to the top of the fence from the inside. It must have been as startled to see me as I was to see it, because it yowled. From inside the apartment came an earsplitting scream. I screamed, too, and my foot slipped. I felt the flowerpots underneath me start to tip. I clutched at the top of the fence, but my hands just slid down the rough wood and I crashed to the ground in the midst of broken pots and dirt and a clatter that seemed loud enough to raise the dead.

I must have hit my head, because everything went black for a minute, as if somebody had turned the lights out. And then I blinked a couple of times and the sun was back. That, and a dark blob close to my face. I blinked some more and saw that the blob was another face. It was very wrinkled. There was a mole next to the narrow nose. I saw white hair and a pair of vibrant violet eyes. The word boomed in my head like thunder—*witch*.

15

———————●———————

Violet eyes. I had never seen violet eyes before. I blinked again. The violet eyes were full of concern. Not wickedness, not evil. Concern.

"Are you hurt?" a voice asked. It was an old voice, but strong. There was concern in the voice, too. "Can you move?"

I tried to nod my head, but it hurt. And then I discovered the other pain—in my right ankle. It seemed to rise up and fill my whole body. It was hot and sharp and terrible. I blinked again. "I—my—I—" That was as much vocabulary as I could manage.

"Barnaby!" the voice called. "Come out here and help!"

121

And then Barnaby was there, leaning over me, peering into my face. Barnaby. Not, as far as I could tell, cursed or spelled or hurt in any way. There was an enormous cookie sticking out of his mouth. "Mmmph," he said.

A wrinkled hand snatched the cookie from his mouth and stuffed it into the center pocket on the front of his overalls. "Help me get her up," the old voice said. "She's sprained her ankle. You take her hand on that side."

"Hi, Casey," Barnaby said, grinning down at me.

The next few minutes were all about hurting. Pulling on my arms, they got me to a sitting position, and finally up on my left leg. But when I tried to touch my right foot to the ground, the pain was so bad that everything started to go dark again. Somehow, with the old woman's arm around me from one side and leaning on Barnaby's shoulder on the other, I got through the gate in the fence, across a flower-lined, stone-flagged patio, through a pair of sliding doors, and onto a big raggedy couch inside.

The delicious smell was coming from here, all right. When they'd settled me on the couch with my right foot propped up on two tattered cushions, I leaned back and took a deep, deep breath. Definitely chicken—and something else. In spite of the pain in my head and the throbbing in my fast-swelling ankle, my mouth began to water.

The woman stood in front of me, her head cocked, the concern still obvious in those strange eyes. She was dressed in a long orange knit dress with sashes of yellow and brown and green at the waist and a huge paisley scarf with long orange fringe tied around her shoulders. "I'm Clarinda McIntosh," she said.

"And she's a really and truly witch, Casey." Barnaby dragged the cookie out of his pocket and took a huge bite. "A good one," he said around the mouthful.

The woman laughed. The white hair that was piled high on her head bobbed. "Only in the sense that herbal healers used to be called witches." She gestured behind her with one hand. I looked over her shoulder into a cluttered kitchen. Above the counters on one side was a wall of open shelves, lined with bottles and jars. Hanging from the ceiling were big bunches of dried leaves and flowers. "Those are for healing."

Barnaby looked up at the woman and smiled his most winning smile. "Poo-doo needs another cookie."

"Poo-doo has already had two more than he needs," she said. "We've got to do something about your friend's ankle. It's puffing up like a balloon." She tilted her head and squinted her eyes. "Mullein," she said. "I picked some mullein just last week. This time of year, the leaves—"

She was interrupted by a piercing shriek that startled me so that I practically levitated off the couch. It rose higher and higher and then dissolved into screeching,

123

raucous laughter. Neither Clarinda nor Barnaby seemed to notice the racket particularly. "What—?" I started to ask. Then I saw. In the corner near the sliding glass doors, standing on a fat T-shaped perch with silver cups at each end, was an enormous blue and yellow and white bird with a long tail and a huge curved beak. He raised his wings and laughed again.

"Don't mind Percy," Clarinda said. "Macaws are all loudmouths. He's managed to get us kicked out of five apartments since he came to live with us. But I know the owner here, so we're okay, aren't we, Perce?"

As Clarinda turned to go into the kitchen, a gigantic fluffy orange and white striped cat appeared around the corner of the couch and leapt into my lap, nearly knocking the breath out of me. It must have weighed twenty pounds. It touched its nose to mine, stared at me for a moment with its golden eyes, said, "Mrrrow," and then settled itself against my stomach, its nose tucked under the end of its tail.

"That's Leo," said Barnaby. "Poo-doo likes Leo." He knelt beside the couch to pet the cat. A rumble like a jet engine began and it seemed the whole couch was vibrating. "We both like Leo. But we don't like Circe. Circe hisses."

"Now *there*'s a witch!" Clarinda said from the kitchen. "That's why I sent her outside. She took an instant dislike to Poo-doo, didn't she, Barnaby? She tried to scratch his nose."

I shook my head. Maybe none of this was real. Maybe I was still lying on the ground among the shattered flowerpots—unconscious. Except the throbbing in my ankle—that was real. That was very, very real.

Ten minutes later, the throbbing was gone. Clarinda McIntosh, good witch, or healer, or whatever, had wrapped my ankle with big yellowish leaves and then with a warm, wet flannel cloth. And little by little, the pain had gone away. Then she had given me a cup of hot, good-smelling tea with a strange flowery flavor that had a little bite to it, and absolutely the most scrumptious cookie I had ever tasted in my life.

I forgot to be afraid. I forgot to ask how Barnaby had gotten there. And I forgot all about Mackenzie and the pet shop and the police.

16

———————●———————

"And then I began my career as a sculptor."

"What's a scup-ter?" Barnaby asked.

"A person who builds things out of clay."

"*I* do that," he said. "I built a whole castle out of Play-Doh."

Barnaby was sitting cross-legged on the floor, with a gray and white kitten asleep in the space made by his legs. He was being very still. Clarinda sat in front of Percy's perch in a padded rocker that was draped with a green and white crocheted afghan in an odd, distorted checkerboard pattern. I was still on the couch with my foot up, holding my second cup of tea. The pain was gone and I was feeling warm and calm and mellow, as

126

if I were adrift on a quiet summer lake, just listening to their voices.

I gazed around the room. It looked like an overstuffed art museum. The walls were covered with pictures, oil paintings and watercolors. I don't know much about art, but they didn't look very good. There was a strange brownish red horse whose legs looked as if they'd been put on backward. And a sailboat that seemed to be perched on the edge of a purply-blue ocean instead of sailing in it. Between the pictures, there were other hangings—dusty macramé pieces with odd bits of shell and feather and sticks stuck into heavy knots, not quite rectangular pieces of handwoven cloth in strange mixtures of colors.

On the wide coffee table in front of the couch, on the tall, spindly-legged table next to the rocker, and among the books on the bookshelves against the far wall stood warped ceramic pots and pitchers with blotchy glazes and sharp-looking edges. There were human figures in awkward poses and animals that were impossible to identify.

"It's my nature," Clarinda was saying, "to be an artist. It's in my blood and bones." She pushed at the strand of hair that had worked loose and was falling over her forehead. "It's just that I haven't quite found my métier."

"What's meh-tee-yay?" Barnaby asked.

I smiled sleepily. I knew the word. "It means the

work she's best suited to do," I explained.

Clarinda nodded at me. "Very impressive, Casey. Are you feeling better now?"

I nodded. I was definitely feeling better—warm and comfortable and drifty. The cat was still in my lap, his purr a deep, calming rumble. "Terrific tea," I said.

"Yes," she said. "Just what you needed. Chamomile, hibiscus, a touch of mint, and the merest whisper of henbane."

Henbane. *Henbane*. Through the soft, warm sleepy feeling came a twinge of something else. There was something about henbane—something wrong with having it in my tea. I peered into my cup. What was it about henbane?

"It acts as a sedative," Clarinda said then, "if used in the proper amounts. Tiny amounts. Of course, like many other strong medicines, it can be dangerous in inexperienced hands. Poisonous, in fact."

I looked up. The violet eyes met mine and the wrinkled skin around them wrinkled even more as she smiled. "Don't you worry yourself about the henbane, my dear. I've been using herbs for fifty years and never lost a patient yet. Now"—she looked at Barnaby— "where was I?"

"You were being a scup-ter."

"Oh yes. Well, look around. I worked very, very hard for a long time. But things didn't turn out the way I saw them in my mind. Sculpture was not what I was meant to do, either." She gazed off into the distance for a moment. Then she shook herself slightly. "But now I may have found it at last—the art form I was born to pursue." She smiled at Barnaby. "You're part of it, young man."

Barnaby straightened his back the way he did when he was being the general. "Me?"

"Yes, you. Last spring I enrolled in a correspondence course. You, Barnaby Dawkins, are my fourth assignment."

"Me?" Barnaby said again, and squirmed so that the kitten woke up for a moment, stretched out one gray paw and yawned, and then closed its eyes again.

"I'm going to write children's books," Clarinda said. "And you will be the main character in my very first one."

"Children's books?" I said.

Clarinda nodded and pushed herself awkwardly to her feet. Though her eyes were sparkling, her body looked old and sore and stiff. "A touch of arthritis," she said. "When I've finished a full course of devil's claw root, I'll feel a little more spry. It's worse when I've been sitting. Now"—she turned to Barnaby—"do you want me to read to you about yourself? I was supposed to observe a child I didn't know and write a description in five hundred words. That was assignment number four. I'm afraid I got a little carried away. I have nearly ten pages on you now."

Before Barnaby could say anything to that, the door-bell rang with a clear double chime. Percy spread his wings and shrieked.

"Hush yourself, Percy," Clarinda said sternly.

Percy laughed a long, loud laugh and then hushed. He lifted one leg and picked at his claw with his enormous beak.

The doorbell rang again, and Clarinda went to answer it. Before she opened the door, she turned and spoke fiercely to the floor near her right foot. "Stay, Poo-doo. And don't bark."

Barnaby grinned and petted the kitten in his lap.

"Mrs. McIntosh!" I heard a deep, surprised voice say as the door opened.

"Joe, isn't it?"

"Right. Joe Rinaldo."

"Well, come in, Joe. And you must be Mackenzie. Come in."

Suddenly, the small room seemed jammed to the walls as a tall, broad-shouldered policeman with blond hair followed Clarinda in. Behind him came Mackenzie. Her eyes widened with shock when she saw me. Barnaby gently pushed the kitten out of his lap, got up, and ran to Mackenzie. He threw his arms around her knees.

"Barnaby," she said, clutching him by the shoulders. "Are you all right?"

He grinned up at her. "Clarinda makes the goodest cookies in the whole wide world."

Before anyone could say anything else, a loud buzzing sound erupted in the kitchen. "My parsley chicken pies!" Clarinda said. "Excuse me for a moment, won't you? I just have to take them out of the oven."

The policeman moved so that Clarinda could get into the kitchen area. He stood then, looking around in obvious bewilderment. He turned on Mackenzie. "*This* is the kidnapper you were after? The witch? The dangerous child abuser and psychopath? Mrs. McIntosh?"

Mackenzie just stood there, looking from Barnaby to me to the policeman. "I—I—"

Percy raised his wings and let out one of his best shrieks. Mackenzie yelped, saw where the sound was coming from, and sat down on the couch very suddenly, barely missing my propped-up foot.

Clarinda came back from the kitchen, seeming to bring with her a new wave of the rich chickeny smell. "Now, Joe Rinaldo, what can I do for you? I suppose Mackenzie thought the general here had been snatched?"

"She was pretty concerned about him."

"And well she should be. I found him, all by himself—"

"I was not by myself," Barnaby put in.

"Sorry. I found him with his faithful dog, Poo-doo."

131

She pointed to a spot on the floor near the policeman's leg. He looked, glanced up at Clarinda, looked back, and shook his head. "They were just about to cross Monument Avenue *by themselves.*" She frowned meaningfully at Barnaby.

"Poo-doo wanted to go to the park," Barnaby said. "I was only taking him. I know the way." From the tone of his voice, it was clear he'd been scolded for this behavior already.

"I was hurrying home to put my pies in the oven, so after he sicced Poo-doo on me and I managed to convince him I wasn't going to feed him gingerbread and then eat him, I brought him with me. He couldn't remember Mackenzie's telephone number, so we called his mother and left a message on her answering machine."

"And who is this?" Joe Rinaldo asked, pointing at me. "Looks like you've had a full morning rescuing kids."

"I'm Casey," I said. "Casey Corrigan. I sprained my ankle."

"So I see." Joe Rinaldo sniffed. "Parsley chicken pie. That's my all-time favorite, Mrs. McIntosh. Are those for Over the Rainbow?"

"Over the Rainbow?" Mackenzie asked, looking up. It was clear she wasn't entirely over her shock. Her eyes looked glazed. "The health-food store?"

Clarinda smiled. "I make all their baked goods for them. Fridays and Saturdays, I fix supper dishes so people can just come in and get something fast but nutritious to take home." She looked up at the clock. "They'll be here to pick up the pies in about half an hour."

Joe Rinaldo put a huge hand gently on Clarinda's shoulder. "This woman is nature's answer to fast food. Parsley chicken pie's my favorite. And Zeus cookies." He grinned and suddenly looked about Barnaby's age. "Especially Zeus cookies." She nodded, removed his hand from her shoulder, and went back into the kitchen.

He looked around the apartment again. I was sipping my nearly cool tea. Barnaby was down on his hands and knees with the gray kitten. Mackenzie sat like a zombie next to me. "Looks like I'm not needed here, after all," he said. "I'd better get myself back to the station." He looked sternly at Mackenzie. Now he looked very much like a policeman. "You'd better be more careful with your accusations in the future. Child abuse and kidnapping are serious business. You could get someone in serious trouble—yourself included."

Clarinda came back, holding up a handful of cookies. She handed Barnaby one. "Break a piece off for Poodoo," she told Barn. "He doesn't need a whole one." She put the rest of the cookies into Joe's hands. "Take these to keep up your strength on the way back to the station," she said.

"Zeus cookies!" he said, his face going all soft again. "Thanks, Mrs. McIntosh."

"Clarinda," she said.

"Clarinda," he repeated, and popped a whole cookie into his mouth.

As Clarinda went with Joe Rinaldo to the door, I held up my cup to show Mackenzie. "Want a sip? It's henbane." I grinned. "It's terrific!"

17

———•———

As Joe Rinaldo started out, someone from the health-food store arrived to pick up the parsley chicken pies. Clarinda went out with him to supervise the loading.

"Henbane?" Mackenzie said. She scooted forward to the edge of the couch, looking around her with suspicion. "Are you nuts? Just because she's got that policeman fooled doesn't mean she's not a witch. Henbane's poison!"

I nodded. "So is digitalis. It comes from deadly nightshade, and it's a terrible poison, but people with heart problems take it all the time. I read that in the witch gardening book, too, the one that told about henbane." I finished the last sip of my now-cold tea. "Even aspirin can kill you if you take too much of it. Clarinda's okay, Mackenzie. Nobody who makes sculpture as bad as that"—I pointed at a figure that looked like a cross between a pig and a giraffe—"can do magic."

Barnaby looked up from playing with the kitten. "Clarinda's a *good* witch, 'Kenzie. She gave Poo-doo his own bowl of water. And cookies."

"Cookies!" Mackenzie snorted. "That's the oldest trick in the world. She probably put something in them. Some kind of drug or something." She turned on Barnaby then. "Why did you leave the yard? You knew perfectly well you were supposed to stay there."

"Poo-doo got out of the fence. He wanted to go to the park."

"Then it's Poo-doo who needs a spanking." She looked around as if to find the dog.

Barnaby grinned. "He went outside with Clarinda."

"And don't you ever, ever, *ever* go anywhere with a stranger again," Mackenzie told him.

"She wasn't a stranger," Barnaby said, his lower lip stuck out. "She was the lady from the park."

"And she's nice, Mackenzie. Really she is," I said.

"What about my feelings?" Mackenzie stood up and Percy squawked at her. She sat back down. "I felt something evil about her the first time I saw her."

"That wasn't psychic. That was just ordinary suspicion, because she was watching Barnaby. But it was a mistake. She was doing an assignment. She's taking a

136

course to be a writer." I looked again at the pig/giraffe. "I hope she writes better than she sculpts."

Mackenzie shook her head. "Yeah, and what about the witch stuff? What about devil's claw root and parsley and—"

"Devil's claw root is for arthritis," I said. "She's not a witch; she's a healer. And it works. She wrapped my ankle in leaves and it doesn't hurt anymore. Look—the swelling's going down, too."

I lifted my leg to show her. Mackenzie sighed. "I don't understand it. My feelings have never been so wrong before." She put her head in her hands.

Clarinda returned just then. "Barnaby Dawkins," she said as she came in, "you've got to work on that dog's manners. Poo-doo tried to get at the pies while Greg was loading them. And when we shooed him out of the car, he growled at us. He actually showed his teeth!"

Mackenzie looked from Clarinda's face to Barnaby's and back. She shook her head.

Barnaby grinned, a sly three-year-old grin. "Maybe he needs another cookie."

"He needs discipline! Too many cookies, even Zeus cookies, are very bad for a dog. Besides, it was the chicken pie he wanted. And since it's nearly lunchtime, maybe he should have some. And the rest of us, too. Luckily, I always make extra for myself while I'm baking. Girls? Barnaby? Would you like to share a little lunch?"

"I have to call my mother," Mackenzie said stiffly. "She'll be worried about us."

I groaned. I'd forgotten all about Mackenzie's mother. We'd rushed out of the house with the linguine in the oven. And there was still all that work that needed doing for Mr. Sternhagen's buffet that night.

"You'd better call Barnaby's mother, too, and leave a new message on her machine," Clarinda said. "Let her know you're with him and everything's fine."

So Mackenzie made the calls. First, she called her mother. Though she was clear in the kitchen, where the wall phone was, I could hear her mother's voice coming through the receiver. That, and Mackenzie's face, let me know that Mrs. Brewster was not happy. "We can't," Mackenzie said into the phone after a few minutes. "Casey hurt her ankle and she can't walk."

There was another torrent of words at the other end of the line. Mackenzie winced, gave her mother the address, and hung up. "She'll be here in a few minutes," she said.

"What about the linguine?" I asked.

"Turned to charcoal," she said. "She thinks she'll even have to throw away the pan."

18

———————•———————

While we waited for Mrs. Brewster, Clarinda was busy in the kitchen, setting out plates for each of us on the long counter, cutting pieces of the parsley chicken pie she'd kept for herself, pouring glasses of milk for us. The smell, which had always been wonderful, got even richer and more wonderful when she cut the pie. Barnaby had abandoned the kitten and was following her around the small kitchen, constantly getting in her way.

"What's in that?" Barnaby asked when she put a piece of the pie on the plate she had said was his. "Is there tofu?"

"Mercy no," she said. "Chicken and vegetables, parsley, fresh mushrooms—"

"Toadstools, more likely," Mackenzie muttered under her breath. She was standing by the double doors, as far from Percy as she could get, frowning out into the small backyard.

"I like tofu," Barnaby said. "And tofu chocolate. That's candy, but it's good for you."

Clarinda laughed. "Don't let anybody fool you, General. Not everything you find in a health-food store is health food. Tofu chocolate is candy. Plain and simple."

"Seaweed's good for you. 'Kenzie's mother says so. 'Cept it tastes yucky."

Clarinda came around the end of the counter and looked at Mackenzie and me. "Who's been giving this child seaweed?"

I waited for Mackenzie to answer. But she just stared out the doors. So I explained about Unicorn Catering and trying to find recipes for customers who wanted health food that tasted good.

The doorbell rang. Percy shrieked and flapped and Mackenzie jumped.

"That's 'Kenzie's mother," Barnaby announced.

"Quiet down, Poo-doo," Clarinda said. "I'm getting it."

I began to think I was going crazy. I could almost hear Poo-doo barking myself.

Mrs. Brewster came in, and I could tell right away that she really was over the edge. When a person as strong and together as Mackenzie's mother goes, it happens fast—like a building being blown up. Her hair was flying, her eyes were wild, and she jittered from one foot to the other as Clarinda welcomed her and asked whether she'd had any lunch yet.

"No time!" she said. "I don't mean to be rude. Thank you so much for what you did for Barnaby and the girls, but I've got to get back to—" She stopped. She took a deep breath. "What is that divine smell?" she asked.

"Parsley chicken pie," Clarinda said. "Whole-wheat crust, low-cholesterol, positively delicious parsley chicken pie. Are you sure you couldn't stay just long enough to have a little taste?"

So we all had lunch in Clarinda's cluttered apartment, Mackenzie and her mother and me on the couch, Clarinda on her rocker, and Barnaby on the floor. While he ate, he fed bits of the pie Clarinda had put down for Poo-doo to the kitten, to Leo, and, when the door had been opened to let her back in, to Circe, who turned out to be perfectly well behaved as long as she was being fed. Percy ate peanuts and occasionally burst into screams of hysterical laughter. The rest of us were used to it by then, but Mrs. Brewster nearly dropped her plate the first time.

Mackenzie, after a couple of suspicious, tentative bites, gave up and ate the pie that was every bit as delicious as the smell and Clarinda had promised. But her frown didn't go away.

"Low-cholesterol?" Mrs. Brewster said, wiping her

141

mouth with a napkin and looking at the empty plate in her lap.

"And low-fat," Clarinda said. "Low-sodium, too. My own recipe. It sells very well at Over the Rainbow. People seem to like it."

"I have a bit of a problem. I don't suppose you'd be willing to—"

Clarinda waved one wrinkled hand. "Of course I would. I've already sent off the ones I baked this morning. But if you'd like, I'd be happy to help you make some more for your buffet tonight."

Mrs. Brewster smiled. Her eyes lost their hunted look. "You don't happen to be a mind reader, do you?"

"I do have a small gift along that line," Clarinda said. "But Casey told me about the business. And the baked linguine."

"Baked carbon," Mrs. Brewster said. "I was going to have to make a new batch and serve it tonight, without so much as a taste test. I figured by midnight tonight, I'd probably be finished in this town forever."

"Help me clear things up here first and then have a nice calming cup of tea. Then we'll go to your place and make up as many pies as you'll need. We can stop for supplies on the way. Barnaby!" Barnaby looked up. He had emptied both plates and was on his hands and knees now, trying to lift the kitten onto Leo's back. "Take Poo-doo out for a little walk in my yard. Mrs.

Brewster says your mother should be back soon. We're going to take you home."

Barnaby put the kitten down. He sat on the floor and folded his arms across his chest. "I'm not going home," he said. "I'm going to stay here forever and ever."

"Don't be silly," Clarinda said. "I'm an old woman. Far too old to take care of a child. That's Mackenzie's job. Besides, your mother needs you at home."

"She doesn't need me," Barnaby said. "And she doesn't like animals. I wanna stay here with Percy and Leo and—"

"Mackenzie—" Clarinda said.

"General Barnaby!" Mackenzie set her empty plate on the coffee table next to the pig/giraffe. "The commander in chief wants you to report to your home base. That's a direct order. You and Captain Poo-doo are wanted there. Do you read me?"

Barnaby frowned. But he unfolded his arms.

"Take Circe out with you," Clarinda said. "And the kitten may go, too, if you'd like. But you have to watch to be sure she stays inside the fence."

Barnaby's face lightened. He got to his feet and snapped a crisp salute.

So Barnaby went outside and Mackenzie's mother and Clarinda went into the kitchen to do the dishes and talk about health foods and recipes and Unicorn Catering. Mackenzie and I were left alone on the couch.

143

Leo jumped up and settled himself on Mackenzie's lap.

"I can't understand it," Mackenzie said in a low voice. "I've been trying ever since I got here to get that feeling back. And I can't. It's gone. When I focus on Mrs. McIntosh—"

"She likes to be called Clarinda," I said.

"When I focus on Clarinda, all I get are good things now. Maybe it's the pie."

I shook my head. "It's not the pie, Mackenzie, it's Clarinda. You said yourself, psychic messages are hard to understand sometimes. You must have just misunderstood."

Mackenzie's face clouded up as if she was going to cry. "I've lost my powers, Casey," she said. "What I saw today turned out to be *wrong*. Barnaby wasn't at the pet shop. Or anywhere near the health-food store. What I saw was wrong! Completely wrong!"

I thought back to that moment in the backyard when we found Barnaby's amulet and we were both so scared. She had closed her eyes and concentrated, and then said, "She's got him." "You weren't wrong," I said. "You saw the two of them together. They *were* together."

"Yeah, but they weren't at the pet shop."

"Mackenzie, you didn't *see* the pet shop. You saw lots of animals. And a big bird. Look around you." She looked up at Percy, who had his head twisted under one wing, picking at something with his beak. She looked

144

down at Leo, purring thunderously in her lap. "Lots of animals! And you saw bottles and jars in the background. Shelves of herbs and spices. Well? Look out there."

Mackenzie looked toward the kitchen and her eyes widened. "That's it, Case. That's just exactly what I saw! Exactly! I even saw the bunches of dried stuff hanging from the ceiling."

"*I'm* the one who said it was the pet shop. And the health-food store."

"I didn't remember those hanging things from the health-food store, so I just ignored them."

"You thought they were part of the static, because you didn't understand the message."

Mackenzie was grinning. "So what I saw was *right*."

I was almost as excited as she was. It proved the truth of her psychic powers once and for all. She'd seen the kitchen in her psychic vision, and she'd never been in this apartment before in her life. "Your pictures were right. It was my interpretation that was wrong."

Mackenzie straightened up suddenly, and Leo, who had seemed sound asleep the moment before, leapt off her lap and landed on all fours next to the coffee table. "Casey!" Mackenzie said. "The witch and Mom!" She was looking out toward the kitchen, where a dark head and a white one were bent close together over a notebook stuffed with cards and bits of paper. "Clarinda knows all about cooking healthy foods. That's why tonight's going to be a success. The double rainbows. Unicorn Catering's going to make it!''

By the time the lunch cleanup was done, I was able to stand on both feet with only the faintest twinge from my twisted ankle. Clarinda promised Barnaby he could come and visit Percy and the cats as often as he wanted. "And have cookies?" he asked.

"One for you and one for Poo-doo on each visit," Clarinda promised. "If you're very, very good."

Clarinda made certain the cats were all inside, turned out the lights, and took her big black bag and her floppy purple hat off a hook near the door. She pulled the hat down over her white hair. Then she held the apartment door open for us.

Mrs. Brewster shepherded Barnaby and Poo-doo through. Mackenzie, who was in front of me, didn't move. She just stood there, staring at Clarinda. "It's the hat!" she said suddenly. "There's something evil about that hat."

19

———————●———————

Mrs. Brewster and Barnaby came back inside. Clarinda put down her bag and took off her hat. Mackenzie stood for a moment, very still, looking at her. Clarinda put the hat back on.

"It is!" Mackenzie said. "It's the hat. When you put it on, I have a perfectly terrible feeling of evil. And when you take it off, the feeling goes away."

Clarinda took the hat off again. Her hair had begun to come loose and wisps of it drooped down to her shoulders. She looked at the hat curiously. "I've never heard of an evil hat."

"Mackenzie," Mrs. Brewster said. "You did say that Mrs. McIntosh—"

147

"Clarinda," Clarinda put in.

"Clarinda is the person you thought was a witch?"

"She *is* a witch," said Barnaby. "A good—"

Mackenzie nodded. "Every time I meditated about her, I kept getting that image. The purple hat. And the word *witch* every single time. I tried it over and over again. The purple hat and the word *witch*. And that feeling of evil."

"And then we saw her buying parsley," I said. "And henbane. And I found a book that said those were herbs that witches used. So it all fit."

"Everything else I felt and saw turned out to be true!" Mackenzie said. "So I don't understand. I still get those feelings—but only when you put on the hat."

"Purple," Mrs. Brewster said. "Purple witch." She started to laugh. She laughed harder and harder, till Percy raised his wings and joined her. We all just stared. "Purple witch! Mackenzie, don't you remember?"

"Remember what?"

Mrs. Brewster stopped laughing then, a puzzled look on her face. "But you couldn't remember. I never said it out loud. Dr. Antoine warned me never to say anything bad about either of them. For your sake."

"Either of who?" Clarinda asked, looking as confused as I felt. "Of whom?"

"Her father or her stepmother. It's a long story, I'm afraid. Mackenzie, think about Eileen."

Eileen, Mackenzie's stepmother, the woman from "News at Noon." The woman who'd just been promoted to weekend anchor. I remembered the way I'd seen her just before Mackenzie turned off the television. Blond hair, perfect teeth, purple silk blouse.

"Purple!" Mackenzie said. "Eileen always wears purple."

Mrs. Brewster nodded. "It's her trademark and good-luck charm. Purple blouse, purple blazer, purple scarf. She never goes on the air without *something* purple. When your father first left, I got to thinking of Eileen as the purple witch."

"Purple witch," Mackenzie whispered.

"But I never said it out loud," Mrs. Brewster said. "I'm sure of it. I promised your therapist I wouldn't."

Clarinda looked at Mackenzie. Her violet eyes reminded me of Mackenzie's, penetrating and intense. "It's the real thing," she said. "You have a bit of the real thing."

"What thing?" Barnaby asked. "What thing?"

"Mackenzie has the gift," Clarinda said. She turned to Mrs. Brewster. "You didn't need to say it out loud. She just picked it up. I take it you don't like Eileen." This was directed at Mackenzie.

"You mean Mackenzie gots a present?" Barnaby asked. "I want one, too. I want a present. Poo-doo wants a present."

"*Like* Eileen? She broke up our family," Mackenzie

149

said. "She took my father away and made us poor and ruined everything. She wrecked our whole lives."

"Reason enough to think of her as evil," Clarinda said, nodding. She looked from Mackenzie to her mother and back to Mackenzie. "Though I don't see any wrecked lives here."

"*Poo-doo wants a cookie!*" Barnaby shouted in frustration.

"Poo-doo is going home," Mrs. Brewster said. "Along with Barnaby. It's high time both of you had a nap."

"Purple witch," Mackenzie said. And then she laughed. "Eileen, the purple witch."

"I wish I'd never thought the words," her mother said.

Clarinda pulled her hat back down over her mussed hair. "Don't wish that," she said. "Without the purple witch, we wouldn't be together here now. There is magic and there is magic."

20

———————●———————

Clarinda turned out to be better than a good witch. As Mrs. Brewster said, she really did have the soul of an artist. She'd found her art form years and years ago, except that she didn't know it. Her art form was food. Cooking, which she'd thought of all her life as just a job she did to support herself while she searched for her métier, had been her métier all the time. Clarinda says Mrs. Brewster may be right, but she's keeping on with the course in writing for children—just in case. Barnaby says her first book should be called *Barnaby and the Good Cookie Witch*.

Unicorn Catering keeps getting bigger and better. First, Clarinda became Mrs. Brewster's assistant. And then Mrs. Brewster made Clarinda a partner.

Mackenzie says Clarinda's a lot more than a partner. She's more like a member of the family. And since she has some psychic powers, too, she and Mackenzie have a whole lot in common. Clarinda has warned her to remember how easy it is to misinterpret psychic messages, so she shouldn't jump to conclusions about any of her feelings, good or bad. I feel better, somehow, knowing Mackenzie can make mistakes, just like us normal types.

She has given up the baggy cotton shirts and pants. Now she wears long, flowing knit skirts and tops and lots and lots of sashes and scarves—red and yellow and orange and green and blue and hot pink—every color but purple. She doesn't look any more like the other eighth graders at Maple Park Middle School than she ever did. But nobody cares. Guys still drool, and she still ignores them.

I know Mackenzie still misses her dad a lot. But she says it was dumb to think when he left that their lives were wrecked. "That's giving one man way too much power. We can manage our lives just fine."

Barnaby's mother changed her mind about animals. She got him that pair of black gerbils at the pet shop. They live in a cage in his room, and he's crazy about them. He calls them Hansel and Gretel. Mackenzie says Mrs. Dawkins probably got them because she thought with real animals around, Barnaby would get rid of Poo-doo. But Poo-doo won't go away. Barnaby's too smart for that. Poo-doo still likes Zeus cookies and always gets his share. All of us can just about see him now.

Howie Mankowitz asked me to the midwinter dance and I went. And he still helps me with algebra sometimes. He's lots better than a subliminal tape. I guess I'll never be a math whiz, but there are no more *D*'s.

I'm still visualizing. I'm not sure it works, but there *was* that "Howie, the knight to the rescue" thing. And I visualized success for Unicorn Catering, and they're getting to be just about the most popular catering service in all of southwestern Ohio. So maybe I have some power, too.

Every night before I go to sleep, I put on a tape of Mayan clay flutes and I close my eyes and I make a picture in my mind.

The tall, gorgeous, green-eyed Casey Corrigan flips her long, smooth hair over her shoulder. She glances at her face in the mirror and smiles. She brushes powder across her narrow, slightly turned-up nose, straightens her shirt over her size 34C chest, and saunters casually down the corridor at Maple Park Junior High, her backpack hanging gracefully from one shoulder. Locker doors slam. Heads turn to watch as she passes.

She hears voices whispering on all sides. "Isn't she terrific?" "I wonder if she'd go to the dance with me?" "Is she dating yet?"

She stops. He has come around the corner. They look at each other. He smiles. His deep blue eyes crinkle at the edges. He brushes back a lock of blond hair that has fallen over his forehead. "Casey," he breathes, his voice low and vibrant.

She smiles. "Later, Jonathan," she says. "Later." She walks on.

OBSOLETE